Love in Lingerie

by Alessandra Torre

Love in Lingerie

ISBN Digital: 978-1-940941-85-1

ISBN Print: 978-1-940941-86-8

Formatting: Erik Gevers

Cover Design: Perfect Pear Creative Covers

Cover Image: Adobe Stock

Editing: Madison Seidler

Beta Readers: Marion Making Manuscripts, Proof is in the Reading, SueBee, Wendy Metz, Tricia Crouch

Proofing: Perla Calas

love in LINGERIE

Alessandra Torre

pi love

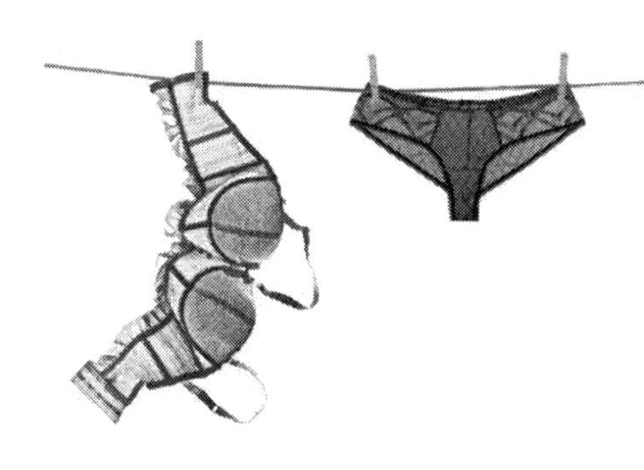

chapter 1
Her

Some men reek of trouble. Trey Marks is one of those men. His fingers haven't stopped moving since I sat down. Right now they are turning the dial of his watch, an expensive piece that peeks out of the edge of his custom suit. I can hear the click of the dial as he gently slides it forward, just one notch at a time, spaced out just enough to drive me mad. Is he even listening to me? I'm barely listening to myself, my ears pricked and tuned to the next click of the timepiece. *Click.*

"If you look at the last page, you can see some of my ideas for your Isabella line…" *Click.*
"I have contacts that could lower your costs, especially in the…" *Click.*
"I'm looking for a position that will allow me to have greater decision-making ability and…" *Click.*

I tighten my hands around the leather portfolio, fighting the urge to reach over and snatch his hands away from the watch. He removes the distraction, the offending hand moving up to rub over his lips. I look away. He doesn't just reek of trouble. The damn man is dipped in temptation, the center of it all radiating out of those eyes. I stepped in this office, and those eyes undressed me. I sat down before him and he all but rubbed his hands in glee.

"You seem apprehensive, Ms. Martin." His hand drops from his mouth and I force myself to meet his eyes.

"I'm sorry. Interview nerves." I smile and he studies me.

"Is that it?" He doesn't believe me. One point for Marks, though I'm not entirely surprised by his ability to read women. His business is seduction, designing lingerie pieces that lure women to purchase and men to take off. According to industry rumors, he's never been married, fucks like an animal, and has a mouth like my shower massager. It doesn't matter. He needs a Creative Director, and I need a new job. Word on the street is that Marks Lingerie is struggling, and I don't need a psychology degree to read the stress that frames his cocky stare. Deep lines across his forehead, the tight clench of his jaw, that damn reach of his fingers to his watch. I recognize the signs. Stress, at the moment, is my life.

It could be worse. I could have a sick child, or an abusive husband—something more valid than the simple fact that I hate my job. I hate it in a way that makes my chest hurt when I step off the elevator each morning. I spend my lunch break in my car, tinted windows up, the engine off, hiding from my bitch of a Creative Director, Claudia VanGaur. She's been threatening to retire for the last decade. For that long, I've been stupid enough to believe her. Now, I'm stupid to stay, stupid to continue waiting for her to turn over the reins. She'll be at Lavern & Lilly 'til she's dead, and torture every employee until that dying breath.

I need a change; I need the promotion I've deserved for a decade. I'll work anywhere in women's fashion, but undergarments are my passion, and this is the first Creative Director opportunity that has appeared in the last year. I don't just want it; I *need* it.

"Tell me about the guy."

"I'm sorry?" I watch as his eyes drop to my hands, to the diamond, and suddenly understand. "Oh. Craig. He's…" My mind blanks. *He's very nice. He's a chemist. He's never looked at me the way that you, right now, are.* "We've been engaged four months," I finish. It's a safe answer, one that doesn't mention Craig's MIT diploma, or his upper-class upbringing. As much as the industry gossips about Trey Mark's bedroom skills, they bemoan his upbringing even more. Raised in South Central. The son of a stripper, one killed in a nineties drug raid. College dropout. The rumor is that he slept his way into some rich old lady's fortune, waited for her to die, then used the ill-gotten inheritance to start Marks.

"Have you set a date?"

With just one question, he exposes everything. "No. Not yet."

"Why not?"

I can feel a scowl forming, the movement of my eyebrows tightening, and I force a smile, letting out a soft exhale as I speak. "We just haven't. We're both very busy right now." I swallow, and hope that I buried the truth. *Because I'm scared. Because I'm bored. Because right now, if I am so easily affected by you, then I probably shouldn't be getting married to begin with.*

His mouth cracks, a widening of lips, the peek of perfect teeth. It is the beginning of a smile, and I can see him fight to contain it, his tongue playing with the corner of his mouth before he purses his lips closed. His eyes drop once more to my ring before they lift again to my face, his features more composed, a flicker of amusement still in those dark eyes. I want to ask him what is so damn funny. Instead, I knot my fingers and focus on finding an imperfection on his face. I fail.

"I'm asking about your fiancé for purely innocent reasons. Kate, I'm not the easiest person to work for." He leans forward, his forearms resting on the desk, and runs the fingers of one hand over the knuckles of his other. "I'm temperamental, and terrible with instructions, and I can be a real asshole." A hint of a smile appears, then he sobers. "But despite what you may have heard about me, there are certain lines I don't cross, and fucking my employees is one of them."

"Literally or figuratively?" I don't know where the words come from, but they are well received, his grin splitting wide open, a chuckle rumbling out.

"Both." He pushes to his feet and extends a hand. "Thank you for coming in, Ms. Martin. Someone will be in touch to follow up."

My stomach twists. Maybe it is my portfolio. Maybe I seemed too eager. Maybe, it is the ring on my finger. I force a smile and slide my palm into his, the squeeze of his handshake just strong enough to ground me. "Certainly. It was a pleasure to meet you."

The lie falls smoothly from my lips, but our handshake lasts a second too long.

I don't know how I'll return to Lavern & Lilly, or how I'll make it through more years under Claudia, but I know one thing: Trey Marks can say all day long he doesn't fuck his employees, but I'd bet you his watch that he'd have spread me wide open on his desk if I'd asked for it.

I push on the exterior door and step into the Los Angeles heat, inhaling the light honeysuckle scent. In four hours, I have dinner with Craig, a meal where he will dissect every moment of my interview and manage to pile more stress onto my job search. I leave Trey Marks's inappropriate comments in the parking lot, and get in my car, my mind already cataloguing which details I will share with Craig.

It takes twenty minutes of windows-down driving, music blaring, my steering wheel shuddering underneath my palms, for me to forget the pull of his smile.

Baby Jesus in a Manger. The man should be illegal.

Him

My desk was a gift from my father, a man who always spent more than he made, my childhood a mix of shiny toys and eviction notices. He gave me this desk a month before he died, the piece plucked from an estate sale down in Rancho Santa Fe, the hundred-year-old piece hand-carved, the edges filled with miniature battle scenes, the top inlaid with leather. I kept the card that he left on its surface, a single notecard, his scrawl barely legible across its lined surface. *Always fight*, it said. An interesting sentiment for a man who drove his brand new Porsche off a Malibu cliff. The responding officers blamed fog and heavy rain. I blamed aggressive creditors, mom's death, and the flask he liked to keep in his front pocket.

I slide the folder of resumes before me, the simple act of opening the folder exhausting in its chore. Staffing will be the death of me. So important to a company, so time consuming when squeezed into a day. But this position, out of all of them, is the most important. I can't pass off my Creative Director to a staffing agency or HR. This role will work hand-in-hand with me. This choice could save Marks Lingerie or cement our demise. I flip through the resumes and stop at Kate Martin's, letting out a stiff breath as I survey the page. A Bachelors from Parsons. UCLA for her MBA. Only one job dotting the work experience section, her last eleven years spent with Lavern & Lilly. I make a face. Lavern & Lilly is conservative women's fashion, its closest competitor White House Black Market. Would she know anything about seduction? About sex appeal? Her conservative pantsuit hadn't exactly helped her cause.

Settling back in my chair, I close my eyes and picture her. Those pale pink lips, a faint tint of gloss, their constant press. She had been nervous, her fingers running over the top of her resume, her hands clenching and unclenching the portfolio, her eyes darting everywhere but my face. I'm not a stranger to nervous women; I've spent a lifetime using my looks to my advantage, my smile and words to fill in any gaps my appeal might contain. If I'd wanted to, I could have had Kate Martin. If I want to, I still could. Fuck the ring and the fiancé. No woman who wants to get married waits to set a date.

"Literally or figuratively?" Something had flashed in her eyes when she had asked the question. The edge of her mouth had curled, the hint of a dimple appearing. In those three words, she had shown what hid beneath that stiff posture and nervous eyes. In those three words, she had shown spunk.

I pull out her resume and close the folder, pushing aside the inappropriate thoughts that have plagued me since our meeting. My company is in trouble. I'm leveraged in ways that make me sweat, our assets dwindling, sales declining, morale at an all-time low. It doesn't matter if Kate Martin is fuckable, willing, or engaged. I don't need another fuck buddy. What I need—more importantly, what my *company* needs—is a savior.

Could she be it?

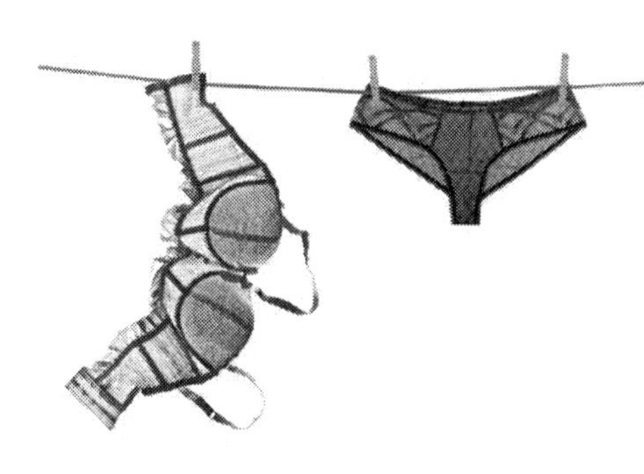

chapter 2
Her

"You got the job? Oh honey, that's terrific!" My mother's voice pumps out from my cell phone, and I can picture her legs moving, one hot pink lycra-ed leg before the other, her free hand swinging, as she moves down the street. "I am *so* proud of you! Do you like your new boss?"

"I'm not sure yet." I open the fridge and stare at the contents.

"I'm sure you will, I can just *feel* it." She inhales. "Plus, it's a new moon tomorrow, and *that* will help." There is the blare of a horn, and the muffled sound of her cursing. I put her on speaker and set the phone down on the counter. When she returns, her voice is bright and cheerful. "So! I'm assuming you gave L&L your two-week notice?"

"I tried. They had security escort me out."

"What?" I can almost hear the screech of her tennis shoes against the pavement.

"It's standard, Mom. They don't want me messing anything up on my way out."

"Well, that's ridiculous. I'm so sorry, Kate." She huffs into the phone.

I find a box of stuffed green peppers in the freezer and pull it out. "Anyway, you can tell Jess tonight. It's not a secret."

"Are you sure you can't come? I've got plenty of food. And you can bring Craig! It'll be fun." Her voice pitches, as if in protest of her words, and I bite back a smile. There are many definitions of fun, but Craig and I—around my sister and her five kids—is never fun, at least not for him. It's entertaining for Jess and me, especially if Mom's pulled out the wine, but it is excruciatingly painful for him. And tonight, as much as I would enjoy seeing them all—I need some space, a quiet night to celebrate my time at Lavern & Lilly, and my fresh start at Marks Lingerie. "Another time. Give everyone a hug from me."

She promises to do so, and I turn on the oven as she hangs up. I call Craig, leaving him a voicemail with the good news, and then I go out to the garage, opening the car's trunk and grabbing the first cardboard box, carrying it into the apartment before returning for the second, and then the third.

Eleven years at L&L and all of it fits into three boxes. I open the first one, and pick through the contents. With the second box, I grab wine and put the green peppers in the oven. Before opening the third box, filled with nostalgia, I eat.

I find a framed photo from just before my Parsons graduation, with my old best friends. Four of us, all with maxed out credit cards and big dreams, clinking sugar-rimmed martini glasses in a dark club somewhere in Manhattan. I haven't looked at the photo in years, and haven't spoken to them in almost that long. Meredith is in Seattle now, Jen is in Miami, and Julie and I got in a fight four years ago and haven't spoken since. I wipe the dust off the frame and return it to the box, not interested in seeing it every day, not interested in feeling the pang of regret. Maybe I should call Julie. I take a long pull of wine and discard the idea. Truth be told, I haven't really missed her.

I sift through a pile of business cards, dropping a few of them into the kitchen trash. Maybe Craig and I can find new friends. He has a group he wants to join—Mensa—and brought home membership tests last week, his application already completed, typed into the form with neat precision. Apparently there are weekly events, parties where intelligence is tested and carefully orchestrated mingling occurs.

I haven't taken my membership test yet. It's an IQ exam, one that ignores any fashion abilities or reality-tv knowledge. Craig has pushed me to take it, sending reminders by email, spare tests brought to every date. I almost took it yesterday, but I'm torn over whether or not to cheat on it. My conscience says no. My common sense says that it's a stupid *Mensa* test and morals aren't really in play, but my fiancé's respect is. On the man's eHarmony profile, he had "intelligence" as his *most* important quality, above cleanliness and personality. Before our first date, he had asked for my GMAT scores. I may have overinflated mine a teensy bit out of competitive pride.

My phone buzzes, and my back stiffens out of habit, my mind steeling for Claudia's voice, before I remember my resignation. I take a long sip of merlot and force myself to relax before I reach for my cell. It's a text from Craig.

Just got your voicemail. Congratulations! Want me to come over to celebrate?

I consider the offer, my eyes moving over the cardboard boxes, the vomit of my past all over the kitchen counters.

Sure. Come over around ten. We can celebrate naked.

I send the message and smile, imagining Craig's face when he reads it, the rise of his eyebrows, the widening of his eyes. It will catch him off guard, our texts never racy, everything appropriate, should anyone pick up either of our phones. But tonight, I'm feeling reckless. Maybe it's the unshackling of my Claudia VanGaur cuffs. Maybe it's the three glasses of wine I've had. Or maybe it's the phantom feel of Trey Marks's eyes, the way that—fully dressed before him—I had felt naked.

I finish off the glass and reach for the bottle.

Craig's knees against the inside of my thighs. His hands beside my shoulders. He dips his head and I lift my chin. We kiss, our teeth bumping, and he slows his thrusts in order to do a better job.

"I love you," he whispers.

"I love you, too." I lift and wrap my legs around his waist, my hands digging into the meat of his ass, and when I pull him hard against me, he responds. There is a moment of heavy breaths and small grunts, and I close my eyes, enjoying the movement, the flex of his cock inside of me, the slap of our bodies together. I can feel when he is close, the quickening of strokes, the tightening of muscles, and he moans, pushing deeper, his body stiffening as he gives one final pump.

I close my eyes, and Trey Marks's face flashes, for a quick moment, in the dark.

At L&L, all of the Los Angeles employees worked in one big loft, our desks arranged in clusters to foster teamwork and interaction. The only thing it fostered was paranoia, the feeling that we were being watched constantly, no conversations private, peak times a shouting match of everyone trying to be heard. Some nights I was hoarse from the constant need to raise my voice just to have a simple conversation.

At Marks Lingerie, I am given a private office, one with glass walls and a view of the city skyline. I run my fingers over my nameplate, the Creative Director title sending a small thread of pleasure through me.

"Got everything you need?" I turn to see Trey, his hand gripping the edge of the doorframe. The tie he wears is crisply knotted, his jacket gone, his short hair styled in the messy way of playboys everywhere. His tan skin contrasts with the blue button-down, his eyes popping against the color.

"I'm good." I smile, pulling my bag off of my shoulder and setting it on the desk. "Great view."

"We need you to keep it." He smiles, and I see the stress behind the words.

"Yes sir." I nod. I can handle pressure. Compared to L&L, this is Disneyland. Instead of eight clothing divisions, we have one. Instead of reporting to Claudia, I've got him.

Lingerie, I can handle. Visions, I can create. A team, I can inspire. A boss, I can please.

I smile at him and can see the worry in his eyes.

It's amazing how productive I am when Claudia is removed from the equation. In a typical day at L&L, I spent five or six hours with her. On my first day at Marks, there was a three-hour stretch where I closed my office door and *no one bothered me.* Total silence! For three hours! I was able to review four years of catalogs and product lines before lunch. I unpacked my thermos and ate at my desk, diving into the designers' files, a task which ate up the rest of the day. I left by six, and was asleep by nine.

On my second day, I conducted an employee survey, as well as interviewed the entire design staff, one-by-one, a process that ate up almost seven hours. The general consensus, though they didn't use these exact terms: Trey is amazing and this job is a cupcake run. Maybe it's the last decade I've spent in cardigan-wearing hell, but my lip had curled a little at the idea of a company drowning, and their employees enjoying the ride. It is past time to rock this boat.

Trey walks by, his jacket on, keys in hand, and I already hate this glass wall that separates my office from the hall. Each pass of his suit reminds me of a donut shop display, a million calories, lined up to tempt you. A million mistakes, all brightly lit and just a touch away. Just before his office, he turns his head, our eyes meet, and it's like biting into a dark chocolate eclair. That one hold of eye contact—it's addictive, the promise of more, the knowledge that you should put it down and walk away.

I've never been good with sweets. If I have one nibble, one bite—I'll eat an entire box. I'll wreck my stomach and destroy my diet, toss away weeks of hard work. I'll give up everything for one long moment of gluttonous satisfaction. I look away, and it is a torturous effort.

It's his fourth pass this morning, his office two doors down from mine. This isn't going to work. Not with a man like him, one too tall to miss, that suit jacket stretching smoothly over muscular shoulders, his dress pants sliding sleekly over what appears to be a perfect ass. God, listen to me. His ass? I've never even noticed a man's ass before. I stand up from my desk before I lose all sense completely. I have four months before I pitch him my vision for next year. Four months to break apart every style line that Marks Lingerie makes and rework it into my own.

The first step to that goal? Remove distractions.

I stand and walk to the corner of the room, then turn back and survey my desk.

Him

She's turned her work station. It's not the first thing I notice when I walk by. The first is her ass. She stands beside the desk, the phone to her ear, and leans forward, her fingers moving on the mousepad, the position serving her body up perfectly. I stop, on my way to the reception desk, a shipping schedule in hand, and can't help but stare.

Long legs stretching up from modest heels. A skirt that starts at the knee and hugs tightly. Her feet are slightly spread, and if I got behind her right now, I wouldn't have to change anything to her position. My hands biting into her hips. That skirt unzipped and puddled around her ankles. Panties pulled aside, cock lined up, her face looking back, eyes on mine.

I force myself to step forward, to put one shoe ahead of the other, the page crumpling in my grip.

  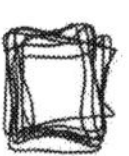

"Explain to me what the fuck you've done." I try to control my voice, try to contain the anger that is rippling through me. The pressure is fucking with my head, it's fraying at my psyche. Three years ago, I would never have lost my cool over this. Three years ago, I would have politely fired the woman and then left the office, the day still bright enough to get in a trip to Malibu. Three years ago, I didn't have the IRS and every bank in town on my ass.

She looks up from her computer and nods toward her door, not one ounce of concern in that pretty face. "Please shut the door."

My hands tighten on the back of the leather chair, one of two that sits before her desk. I straighten, and reach one hand out, the tight quarters making it easy to grab ahold of the door and swing.

Click. The sounds from the office disappear. I turn to face her, and she sits back, her arms crossing over the front of her chest. "I need more clarification. I've done a lot of things."

"I can see that." If she were a man, I'd have her by her throat, pushed up against the wall, so close that our bodies were touching. Maybe it's better that she's not. I'd probably lose focus.

She rolls her eyes as if I don't hold her job in my hands. As if she owns this company, and I am bothering her with my questions. "I don't have time to play games, Trey. What did I do to piss you off?"

I should fire her. Right now. Fire her and spend the rest of the day putting my company back together. My hands find the back of the chair again, and I wrap my palms around it, squeezing hard. "You fired seven people." *Seven.* A third of the design staff.

"My job description states that I can adjust staffing."

"That's not an adjustment, that's insanity."

"It cleared five hundred thousand dollars off of the budget. And I spoke to the design staff about it."

"Which staff?" I think of the seven people on her ax list. Seven lives she just ruined. Would they find new jobs? Would they—

"All of them."

"Twenty-two employees?" Unlikely.

"At ten minutes per meeting, it doesn't take that long. I got in early yesterday and knocked it out. Plus, I used the survey results."

Oh yes. The survey. That had certainly put the department into a state of panic. "That wasn't a survey, it was a witch hunt." The survey had contained only three questions. It had been sent to her team at precisely two o'clock, and a timer had run in the top of the window, giving the participants only thirty seconds to complete the survey. The first question had asked, on a scale of one to ten, how overworked you felt. The second asked which three jobs were expendable in the company. The third asked which three people were expendable.

"Witch hunt or not, the results were fairly clear." She slides a piece of paper forward, one covered in bar graphs and statistics.

"You fired Ginger. She's practically our mascot." Ginger, the seventy-year-old woman who prepared coffee each morning and got everyone's lunch. Her official title was something about quality control.

"Be realistic." She stands up, her steel gaze nothing like the polite interviewee who had quivered before me. "You can't have mascots and people working here just because they are well-liked. You can't have a hundred percent of your employees giving ones and twos on their level of stress." She stabs a finger toward the page. "You are running a business, one that, if we don't turn around, is going to end up firing every single one of them. I *need* you to trust me, and in one year, we'll be giving jobs to a dozen new people. In one year, we will be profitable. In one year, if you want Ginger back, you can have her."

I've never wanted to kiss a woman so badly in my life. To bury my hands in her hair and dominate that mouth. My hands twitch on the leather back of the chair. I stop myself from moving forward and pulling her across that glass desk.

I don't like strong women. I don't like being yelled at. I don't like being proven wrong. She has the data. She's done the homework. I know, I have known, that we are slightly overstaffed. I've known for six months that I should lay off one or two people. Seven people is ridiculous. But half a million dollars is badly needed.

"I didn't hire you to run my business. I hired you for your creative input and vision. I hired you to create products that sell. You have to consult me in these decisions, even if it involves your team." She doesn't understand that this is my family, paychecks I have paid for nine years, lives that depend on me.

"I was typing up a memo when you came in. You'll have it within the hour. It will explain all of the reasoning behind the decisions."

"Next time, get me the memo *before* you fire anyone."

She tilts her head, as if she is *considering* the order. I watch her front teeth bite gently down on her bottom lip, and all I can think about is my cock sliding into that mouth. "I need decision-making ability. It's in my job descript—"

"Job description," I interrupt. "I know." She's obsessed with them. I can see, spread out on the glass top of her desk, a dozen of them, covering different roles in the company. She's probably the only one who has ever read them, much less taken them as gospel. I need to review hers. I have a feeling it will be haunting this relationship. I unwrap my fingers from the chair, and can see the indentations I have left, the bites in the leather, ones that are already beginning to fade. I step back, and notice her heels, lined neatly up by the credenza, her bare feet against the wood floors, the tip of each toe painted a light pink. She has tiny ankles, and I have a brief vision of my hand wrapped around one, her feet against my shoulders, my palm running down the length of her legs.

She raises her eyebrows and I try to find a coherent stream of thought. "I'll be looking for that memo." I stop, one hand on the doorknob, and feel like I'm running. I need to say something else, something that puts me back in the driver's seat and reaffirms my authority.

There is a long beat where her eyes hold mine, a challenge flashing out, clouding the arousal. My dick is confused, and so is my head.

I open the door and escape into the hall, into my domain.

If this woman was lingerie, she'd be black leather, with studs along the seams and enough of a dominatrix vibe to give a man pause.

If this woman was lingerie, I'd strip it off and then properly show her who is in charge.

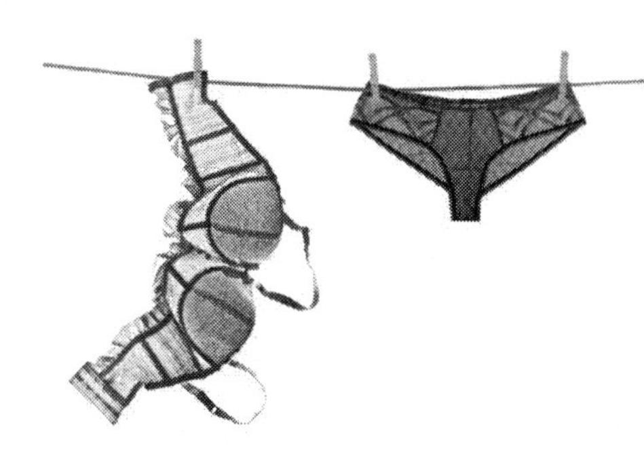

chapter 3
Her

two months later

"I just don't understand how you didn't get it."

I let out a controlled breath, pulling my seatbelt across my chest and pushing it into the clasp. "I'm sorry. I just couldn't figure it out."

Damn Mensa and their "delightfully fun puzzles!"—puzzles that I had failed. We'd had four challenges in tonight's party, and I had failed three of them. Craig was—still is—dismayed by my results. Next week's event is a "fun team challenge!" which I'm assuming will mean that Craig's and my scores will be combined. That possibility seems to be the true root of his panic.

I glance over at him, watching as he flips on the windshield wipers and checks all three mirrors before shifting into reverse. His face is pale blue from the restaurant's sign, the fluorescent neon highlighting the thick mop of dark hair that is perfectly combed, despite the stress of the evening. I consider telling him the truth, and just as quickly discard it.

The truth is, I cheated on the Mensa admittance test. I found an online answer sheet and penciled in enough right answers to get me in, without arising any suspicions over a perfect score. I got my laminated card, slid my hand into Craig's, and walked into that damn event. I didn't think it would be so hard. I didn't realize that everyone would be so freaking serious about the thing. Each challenge had been timed, the correct answers written on a big white board in order of timing. In the air, competitive spirit had almost crackled with intensity. At the end of the night, Craig had placed second. The losers had been on their own board, a board that I dominated in depressingly consistent fashion. The only name lower than mine had been Chad, a scrawny guy with skinny jeans and a pierced tongue. Chad had been brought by his parents, and was a high school sophomore, a fact that Craig had pointed out three times.

"Maybe you have performance anxiety." Craig rolls the syllable of each word on his tongue as if testing their flavors. "Athletes suffer from it all of the time. Maybe it caused your brain to lock up."

"Maybe." I reach down, into my purse, and pull out a pack of gum. "Want some gum?"

"I bet there are exercises we could do online. We could time them, to try to recreate the environment. Or maybe food—you know, tryptophan relieves anxiety."

"Tryptophan?" I pull a stick of Big Red out and hold it toward him, his head shaking subtly, his hands remaining locked in their ten and two positions. "Like turkey?"

"It's a precursor to a neurotransmitter called serotonin, which helps you feel calm."

"I *know* what serotonin is," I say flatly, though—honestly—I don't. I mean, I sort of know what it is. Though I thought it had something to do with sunshine and skin. Or maybe that's melatonin. Or melanin. Something like that.

"It's not just in turkey," he continues, the van coming to a complete stop at a stop sign. There are no cars in sight, not so much as a falling leaf moving, yet he looks left, then right, then checks his rearview mirror. "It's also in chicken and bananas. Cheese, oats, peanut butter…" He continues to list food and I rest my head on the headrest, tuning him out. He's crazy if he thinks that I'm going to do a *food prep* for the next meeting. I'm not even certain I'm *going* to the next meeting. I'm not even home from this one, and I'm already dreading it.

"I've got an early morning tomorrow." I interrupt his continuing list of tryptophan foods, a list that is getting ridiculously long, and I don't know what is more alarming—how many foods contain tryptophan, or how many foods that Craig is aware of. There are times when it is convenient to date a brilliant man. There are other times, present moment included, when it is just really damn annoying. It'd be one thing if he was quietly brilliant, the sort of quiet and unassuming genius that keeps all of his worldly knowledge to himself. But Craig is more of the "let everyone know how much I know" type. He won't shut up about it. And tonight, I can't take any more of it.

"Oh. So … I won't come in, then." He puts the van into park and turns on his hazards, a habit I used to find endearing but tonight is absolutely maddening in its overkill. The chances of someone tearing around the curve and hitting his vehicle in the moments in which he is walking me in … they are minute at best. He waits a beat before opening his door, his head tilting to me, waiting for confirmation of his suggestion.

"That would probably be best." I stuff the gum pack back into my purse, waiting for him to walk around the front of the car, his journey marked by the orange flares of his hazard lights. He opens my door and I step out.

"Tomorrow, we can brainstorm about next week," he says, helping me up the dark path to the building.

"Sure." I'll brainstorm all right. I'll spend every second of tomorrow's spare time devising an excuse for my absence. Maybe a last-minute meeting? Or a highly contagious cold?

We come to a stop outside the door. "Goodnight, Kate." His kiss is soft, a gentle press that speaks of forgiveness. *I forgive you for your terrible performance tonight. I forgive you for your performance anxiety, and for embarrassing me. Next week, we will do better. I know it.* I hear the words as clearly as if he speaks them.

"Goodnight."

It's not his fault I cheated. I unlock the door and wonder how much of my irritation is due to myself, and the un-winnable situation I've put myself in. Once inside, I reconsider inviting him in. Will he be able to move past my performance? Will we be able to discuss *anything* other than that damn whiteboard and his second-place standing on it?

I move down the hall to my apartment, heading for the shower as soon as I step in.

Him

My sex life has occasionally put me in awkward situations. That's what happens when your brand of kink is outside the box. It puts you in unique places, with unique people. This is the first time it's put me in front of a gun.

The setup had been simple, which typically works best in these situations. I leave a key at the front desk. I go to the room. At 10 PM I go into the shower, taking my time. When I finish, and step out, into the hotel room, she will be waiting on the bed. Cue the fun.

She is waiting, all right.

I rest my hands on my bare hips and look past the 9mm, and to the woman holding it. She looks nothing like the profile photos, her hair dark instead of light, her breasts big instead of small, her eyes calculating instead of sweet. She smiles, and a silver tooth glints out from her smile. I hope she's not planning on raping me. I have a wide range of women who I find attractive, but crazy bitch isn't on that menu.

A man comes from behind her and steps past me, into the bathroom. There is the rustle of clothing, and then he emerges, rattling my car keys. "Struck the jackpot with this one," he drawls. "Tesla."

He's an idiot if he thinks that stealing my car is a wise move. The thing is outfitted with enough tracking software and cameras to find Jimmy Hoffa's body. I open my mouth to enlighten them, then shut it. Let them get caught. They'll have to stop and charge the damn thing soon enough, its battery already low. He has my wallet and watch in hand, and I wince at the sight of the Glashutte Original in his hands. The watch was my father's—the inscription imprinted on me, his rough drawl clear as day in my mind every time I read it. *You are the captain of your soul.* The loss of it will hurt more than the car.

"Nice watch." He grins at me and he is lucky I value my life. Take the gun out of this equation, and I'd have him down on the ground, my fist in that smirk, then my elbows. He thinks I am a rich prick who grew up above the law. He doesn't know the neighborhoods I roamed as an only child, the type of streets where you fought for your respect and stole everything else.

Maybe I've gotten soft. I should have left the watch at home. I could have stuck a twenty in my pocket and left the keys in the car, locking it with my phone instead of the fob. Instead, I trusted the address, the Ritz Carlton logo, and a squeaky clean online profile. Now I'm *literally* left with my dick out, watching the man stuff my clothing into a duffel bag, my thousand-dollar jacket shoved, with little regard, in last. I watch my phone disappear into his jean pocket.

"You mind leaving my clothes?" I flash the woman a smile. "It'd be nice to walk out of here."

The grin, one that hasn't failed me yet, earns me a downward glance, her eyes drifting over my cock. "Go right ahead, beautiful. Nothing to be ashamed of there." She smacks her gum and smiles. "Now, let's get your sexy ass on that balcony."

I am half-relieved, half-concerned, at the instructions. Maybe she isn't going to kill me. Maybe she'll just lock me out, thirteen floors up. If so, how long will it take for someone to see me? How long before they track down my room and let me out? I glance toward the balcony door. "Give me a robe, at least."

She considers the idea, then nods, barking out an order to the man, who scoffs at my request while wearing a puffy jacket that I could climb Everest with. I watch as he yanks a fluffy white robe off a hanger and walks past me, giving me a wide berth, the sliding door opened, the robe left outside. Sixty seconds later, I am beside it, the woman's bright orange fingernails waving at me as she closes the curtain and locks the door. I pull on the bathrobe and wonder how the fuck I got here.

"Mr. Marks, you can't throw furniture off the balconies." The hotel's night manager sneers at me with a snobbish scowl that I haven't seen in a decade, not since I moved solidly into the upper class.

"I *understand* that. I was trying to signal to the people out on the deck." In the lunacy of this situation, *I* seem to be in trouble, the man glaring at me as if I am about to be put on a Ritz Carlton blacklist of sorts.

"You will have to pay for the damage. You destroyed the chaise lounge. And the side table." He pushes a piece of paper forward, one where he has neatly written down both items, as if I might argue this point at some future moment. Underneath the two, he has added "Bathrobe: $40," the words underlined.

"That's fine. I'll pay for it." I rub my eyes and wonder at what point everyone lost their damn minds. The police had been the first to show up, called by this idiot, who still seems convinced that I was drunk and slinging furniture off my balcony just for the joyous hell of it. It took fifteen minutes to explain the situation and get them in pursuit of the Tesla, which could be halfway to the border by now. Then, I had to practically beg the hotel for use of their phone, making calls to my credit cards and bank. By the time I hung up with American Express, this vulture was waiting, pouncing on me with the ferocity of a disapproving parole officer.

"We aren't a party hotel, Mr. Marks. We would appreciate it if you conducted such … events at another establishment." *Events*. I'm not sure if he is referring to my sex life or the robbery. I ignore the statement and stand, rubbing my fingers across the lines of my forehead. "I'd like to make a final call, if you don't mind. Then I'll be on my way and out of your hair."

The man purses his lips. "There is the issue of the payment for these items. I'm afraid that you won't be able to leave until they are taken care of."

My patience snaps. "I *told* you that I will pay for them. Just charge them to my room." I reach forward, putting a hand on the phone and dragging it toward me. I need to call someone to pick me up, but all of my numbers are in my phone. I flip the phone book open to the residential section, thinking through my friends, my mind blanking on half of their last names.

"Your card has been declined, sir." I stop somewhere in the Ds, and turn my head to him. "What? It's an American Express. Run it again—" *Oh.* In my haste to stop the bitch from a Trey Marks sponsored shopping spree, I had reported all of my cards stolen. The American Express representative had gone through the pending transactions with me, and I had authorized the hotel's hold on the room. Their initial authorization had probably not been enough to cover the damn furniture, this new authorization rejected.

Fuck. "I'm sorry. I just had all of my cards canceled." I run a hand through my hair and try to think. I hate the look on this asshole's face right now, that mix of pity and contempt, his thoughts as clear as the smell of shit that I have stepped in. *You can't afford to be here. You don't belong here.* Words I've run from for a decade, fought through, moved past with my fucking Tesla and penthouse, my company that I can barely keep afloat. I look down at the phone book and fight the urge to smack it across the man's knowing face. "I'm calling someone to pick me up. They'll pay for the items."

I turn another page, my options reducing.

If this night were lingerie, it'd be a leopard print satin set. Trashy and destined for ridicule.

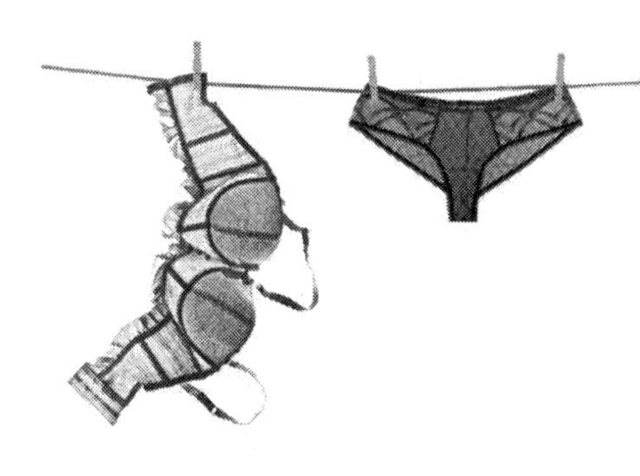

chapter 4
Her

It's my car's first visit to a Ritz Carlton, and I pull up carefully, worried that I might bump into a Rolls Royce or a priceless planter, the deserted drive giving me a little peace. I come to a stop before the valet, who eyes my Kia in the cautious way that someone might avoid a bum. There is a knock on the passenger window and I startle, glancing over to see Trey. I roll down the window, watching his hand steal in and take the leather portfolio off of the passenger seat. "Is this it?"

I nod. "Yes."

He doesn't explain why he needs the company's checks at one in the morning, or why he's wearing a bathrobe. "I'll be right back." He walks off with the portfolio, and I notice his bare feet. In the last two months, I've seen several sides of Trey Marks. This is, by far, the oddest.

Ten minutes and five bucks to the valet later, I pull away from the hotel, the check folder in Trey's lap, the top of one muscular thigh visible under the edge of his robe.

"Where are we going?" The streets are empty, amber streetlights illuminating half moons of asphalt, the bright glare of road construction up ahead.

"Good question." He lifts up a hand and rubs at the back of his neck, a scent of soap drifting over. I've never been so close to him, his elbow bumping against me, his knee close to the gearshift, my movements careful not to touch him. He shifts in the seat and his robe opens further. I get a glimpse of more thigh and flick my eyes back to the road. *I don't think he's wearing underwear.* The questions mount.

He turns his head, and I feel his eyes on me. "Does your fiancé live with you?"

"No." I think back to our disastrous Mensa meeting, the stilted goodbye. Good thing Craig hadn't spent the night. I could explain a lot of things, but a call at one in the morning would be difficult. "Why?"

"I don't have my keys. Maybe we can find a hotel, one that will accept checks." He falls silent, and I attempt to put together the pieces of what he is saying.

"You need a place to stay? Tonight?" I look over. "Is that the roundabout point you are trying to make?"

"I don't want to impose."

I smile despite myself. "You woke me up in the middle of the night and dragged me downtown. Letting you crash on my couch is minor. Yes, you are welcome to stay at my apartment. Assuming of course, that you behave."

He drops his head against the headrest, a low chuckle rolling out. "Trust me, Kate. You have nothing to worry about."

"Thanks." The word comes out tart and offended, as if I want to be pursued, and I struggle to recover.

"I didn't mean it like that." He looks down at his lap and adjusts the white terrycloth. "It's just been one of those nights that makes you want to swear off sex forever."

"I've got to admit, you've piqued my curiosity." I get on the on-ramp. "Girlfriend problems?"

"Something like that." He reaches over and adjusts his air vent. "Can you turn the heat on? I'm freezing."

I glance toward him and turn a dial, increasing the flow of hot air. "Where are your clothes?"

"Good question." He leans forward, holding a hand to the vent. "In my car, along with my phone, watch and wallet. And my condo keys." He frowns. "Can I borrow your phone?"

"It's in my purse. Down by your feet." I tell him the unlock pin and watch as he pulls up the internet, does a quick search, then places a call. I get off on my exit and eavesdrop as he speaks to someone in his building, instructing them to deactivate his key fob.

He ends the call and returns the phone to my purse. "Thanks. I wouldn't have bothered you, but you're the only person I know who is still listed in the phone book."

I grin, the precaution one that Craig had insisted on, and I had always deemed a nuisance. "No problem." As irritated as I had initially been with his middle-of-the-night call, this was turning into one of my most exciting nights in years. "So … is your car back at the Ritz?"

He rubs the back of his neck. "According to the police, it's somewhere in San Diego right now. They're tracking it down." He glances at me. "I was robbed."

"In your bathrobe?"

He laughs, and it's a nice one. Deep and strong, the kind you want vibrating against your skin. "I was naked, actually. The bathrobe was a bit of kindness on their part."

Their part. A robber duo. Or trio? I try to figure out how Trey Marks was robbed while naked at the Ritz Carlton, and come up completely blank. It's like those damn Mensa puzzles. I have all the pieces; they just won't fit together. "I need more information," I say finally, admitting defeat as I bring the car to a stop at a red light.

"I was meeting someone for sex. I left a key at the front desk. They came in when I was in the shower and robbed me." He shrugs off the explanation, as if is a commonplace response, and one that makes perfect sense.

I was meeting someone for sex. I left a key at the front desk. It takes a few seconds for any possibility to come to mind. "Like a prostitute? You were meeting a prostitute?" I feel a burst of excitement, the term for this popping to mind. Rolled. He was a john and got *rolled.* I mentally high-five my super cool trendy self.

He shifts, the vinyl seat squeaking in response. "Sure. If that's how you want to think about it."

"That's a bullshit answer. Either she was a prostitute or she wasn't."

"She wasn't a prostitute." He turns a little in his seat to face me. I successfully resist the urge to check how his new position affects my chance of a penis sighting. He's not wearing underwear. He all but said that. Meaning that there is only a thin bit of terrycloth between us. If I reach over and nudge the fabric, he'll be right there, fully exposed. I focus on keeping the car very precisely spaced in the center of the lane. *She wasn't a prostitute.* Another maddeningly odd puzzle piece.

He clears his throat. "Do I seem like I'd need to pay for sex?"

"No." I could have shouted it through stadium speakers and it wouldn't have been more emphatic. Women probably pay *him* for sex, for the opportunity to sample that mouth and body. I straighten a little in my seat. Maybe that's the answer. "Are *you* a prostitute?"

"God, you're terrible at this game." He looks out the window, eyeing the buildings that pass. "I'm not a prostitute, Kate." He sounds disappointed. "I don't want to talk about it. I fucked up and got burned."

"I can't believe the hotel wouldn't give you any clothes." I also can't believe he didn't *pack* any clothes. I guess whatever he had planned with this non-prostitute visitor—he hadn't planned to spend the night. I guess he just waltzed in with his condom and dick—nothing else needed.

"The gift shop was closed. And the employees were unwilling to part with their own."

I turn off the street and into my apartment's garage, driving to my assigned spot. I shift into park, my hand brushing against his knee, and he moves away from the contact. I turn off the engine, and he unlocks his seatbelt, the sound unnaturally loud.

My couch is a sectional, one that doesn't fold out, and I tuck a sheet under the cushions, moving with quick precision as Trey wanders around the living room, picking up and moving anything that he finds interesting. Craig was the complete opposite the first time he came into my home. He'd hovered by the front door, his eyes darting to me, needing the verbal authorization before he'd felt comfortable enough to fully step inside. Second, he didn't touch my stuff. He *still* asks before picking up a frame, or opening a drawer. I like that, that even now, two years into our relationship, he has respect for my space, for my things. When we move in together, he won't invade, but rather carefully ease in, all the while confirming and diplomatically discussing boundary items like dirty laundry and personal time.

I hear Trey open my bedroom's closet door and I pause, mid-fluff, of a pillow. "What are you doing?" I call out, setting down the pillow and moving into the room.

"Looking for clothes. Where does your fiancé keep his stuff?"

He crouches, moving aside the bottom of an old prom dress, then stands, turning to me, as if he isn't being the rudest person on earth. "Huh?"

"Huh, what?" I cross my arms in front of my chest.

"Where does your fiancé keep his clothes?" He raises an eyebrow and damn, he is beautiful. His robe is open at the chest, showcasing muscles that hug either side of his neck. His chest is bare and tan, the muscles strong and well-developed. He swallows, and I yank my eyes back to his face.

"He doesn't keep clothes here. He packs a bag when he comes." I suddenly think of something. I snap my fingers in excitement and run for my keys. "I'll be right back. I'm going to grab something out of the trunk."

I am at the front door when his hand wraps around my forearm. "Wait." I pause, my hand on the door, and look up into his face. "Let me get it. It's too late for you to go out there alone."

I snort. "I just went out there alone when I went to pick you up. You weren't too concerned about me then."

"Selfish necessity. And I didn't realize the setting. It's too dark of a garage. Too many places that someone could hide and wait for you. Just tell me what to look for."

I yield, glumly handing over my car keys. "In the trunk, on the left side, there are two big ziplock bags. Grab the one labeled 'Craig'."

He nods. "I'll be right back."

When he returns, he hands over the bag, our fingers brushing. I turn away, open the bag above the kitchen counter, and pull out the clothes, an emergency set that Craig had insisted, when we'd first started dating, that we carry in our cars. As he likes to preach, it never hurts to have a spare set of clothes. It's the same reason why our trunks have bottled water and granola bars, first aid kits and flare guns. Once we marry and move to a house, we will have a generator and a storm cellar, fire evacuation plans and enough canned food to get us through a month-long famine. I hold out the clothes. "Here. I can't promise they'll fit."

Trey takes the clothes—a new pair of Wrangler jeans, boxer briefs, and a T-shirt. "Do you mind if I take a quick shower?"

"Sure." I point to the bathroom. "There are towels underneath the sink. Feel free to use the shampoo and soap that's in there."

He goes. The bathroom door shuts and I try not to think about his robe dropping, and Trey Marks standing, fully naked in the space.

I've worked for Trey for two months now. Long enough that I feel comfortable around him, long enough that I no longer flinch when he comes near me. When we bump against each other, when he leans over my desk and examines documents, I no longer hold my breath, or sneak an illicit sniff of his cologne. He treats me with a sort of wary respect, and I've grown confident enough to let my opinions fly, sometimes without an appropriate filter or level of respect. It's not that I don't respect him, it's just that I sometimes forget my place, overly empowered by my position. At Lavern & Lilly, I made decisions, and then waited to be admonished or overruled. At Marks Lingerie, he only watches, his eyes following my every move, my freedom eerie in its entirety. He promised me control over the design team, and he has delivered on that promise. It hasn't stopped his temper from flaring, or arguments erupting between us. In the last two months, there have been plenty of both. *I was meeting someone for sex.* There is a whine of water pressure, and the shower turns off.

I clean off the coffee table and move the remote near his pillow. I consider it, then move it back to the coffee table, lining it up this month's issue of *Vogue*. I should be tired. The last time I was up this late was before Fashion Week, and I fell asleep mid-sketch. It wasn't a graceful slump either. I face-planted into the desk, my hand getting caught in between my body and the desk, my ring finger bending the wrong way. I didn't even wake up from the pain. I woke up an hour later, the imprint of a stapler against my cheek, and when I saw the right angle of my finger, I passed out from the sudden brutality of it. *That* overreaction gave me a black eye, and caused poor Craig a hundred glares.

The bathroom door opens, and I turn. "Oh my God." I lift a hand to my mouth to cover up my grin. "You look…"

"Sexy." He fills in, then cocks his head, as if he can tell he guessed wrong. "Irresistible? Rugged?" He steps forward. "Wait, I got this. Drop—"

"Ridiculous," I interrupt. "And … *big*." Craig would have been appalled at such a kindergarten word, but it fits. He looks like a giant trying to wear a mortal's clothing, the boxer briefs skin-tight, the T-shirt stretched across his chest and ending halfway down his abs. I swallow.

His eyes twinkle. "Why, thank you." He shrugs. "I *have* been told that, on several occasions."

"Not *that*…" I blush. "You know what I meant." But he is big. The underwear that fit Craig so easily are tight around his thighs, the waistband riding low enough on his hips to show me those perfect angled cuts. And the bulge they point to … I turn my back to him and grab a few pillows off the couch, moving them to a basket beside my chair.

"Speaking of size, how big is your fiancé?" I hear a pop of fabric and look back to see him pulling off the T-shirt, his face covered by the white fabric.

I love Craig, I do. It's been a great two years. We are consistently compatible. I wear his grandmother's ring, and get along with his parents. Soon we will get married, and I will have his babies, and we will live out the rest of our lives in orderly, organized, and well-prepared fashion. All that aside, I can't control myself from stealing *one* moment, one literal *second*, and enjoying the beauty that is my boss. It's criminal that God would pair his face with those notches of abs, a neat row of thick muscles that pop and slide under his tan skin. I imagine what it would feel like to run my hand across them, maybe even down them. Would he step closer if I slid my palm inside of those boxer-briefs? Would his eyes close if I wrapped my hand around his cock?

The T-shirt lifts higher and I turn my head back to the basket, my breath hissing through my teeth as I fight to keep from looking at him.

"Well?" He steps closer, and in my peripheral vision, I can see him wad the shirt into a ball.

"What?" I straighten, and push hair away from my face. *I am fine. He is going to bed. Nothing is going to happen.*

"Your fiancé. Clark? How big of a guy is he?"

"His name is Craig." I move past him and check the thermostat, turning it a few degrees cooler. "He's average." Average? Craig would be offended by the term. Then again, I am a wee bit offended from his reaction to my Mensa performance.

"He wears a *medium*." He looks up from his examination of the tag, the word said with repulsion.

"So?"

"No grown man wears a medium." He delivers the statement as if it is fact.

"Some do." I flip on a Scentsy warmer and move to the kitchen, turning on the water and washing my hands. "Would you like anything to drink?"

"I'm good. You can head to bed. I'll be fine." He pauses at my fridge and pulls at the edge of a photo, held in place by a daisy magnet. "Is this you?"

I yank the photo from his hand before he gets too good a look at it. It's one of me and Dad, my freshman year at Parsons, before he got sick. "*Go* to bed." I point to the perfectly made up couch, eight feet away. "Now."

He smiles, and clicks his tongue at me. CLICKS his tongue. I don't know whether to be infuriated or lay back on the counter, begging for that tongue across every inch of my skin. "Submission isn't really my thing, Kate." The words drawl out, and I have no doubt that this man left submission behind in preschool. He probably orders the sun to rise, the traffic lights to change, and if he ordered every woman in America to buy his lingerie, he'd be ankle-deep in business right now. He—

I stop, an idea brewing. Trey Marks, a black and white image, in his suit, a devilish smirk in full effect, sitting in a leather club chair, a whisky in hand. Trey Marks, a high contrast video, him slowly rolling back his shirt sleeves, the tie loosened around his neck, his eyes boring into the camera.

I drop the paper towel on the counter and move past him and to my desk. I steal a piece of paper from the printer and sit down.

drop your pants.
turn around.
let me see you.
**Dress your body in the finest lingerie on Earth.*
**Your body is art. Dress it that way. Let it shine. sparkle.*

"What are you doing?" His hand rests on the desk, and he leans forward, looking at the page. I watch his hand, the flex of minute muscles, the strong and beautiful lines of his fingers. The bare ring finger, the odd look of his wrist without a watch.

I look back to the page, the idea still gaining momentum in my mind. "I don't know yet. I think I have an idea for a new ad strategy."

"We don't have the money for ads." He pushes off the table, the words clipped, and I can feel the disappointment radiating off him.

I turn in my chair and watch him walk away. It's not that difficult of an activity, not when he's in just underwear, his ass displayed to perfection, the lines of his back lean and strong. He needs to put on more clothes. If Craig's don't fit him, he can put the bathrobe back on. Or get under the sheets. I can't possibly come up with a winning strategy while he saunters around practically naked. "We'll find the money."

He doesn't turn. "You've seen the balance sheets. We're barely making payroll."

"Borrow it."

I watch as his hands clench into fists, then relax. "I'm leveraged as much as I can be."

"Then we'll wait until we have some profitable quarters. We *will* be profitable." I believe the words, and if he can't hear that in my voice, he's an idiot. "Don't worry," I add. The poor man. Talk about a rough day. I think of Craig, who is most definitely in bed right now, his noise machine on, the sound of crashing waves floating through his seventy-one-degree bedroom.

"I know advertising isn't my department, but I can design a line around this concept. If—"

"We can discuss it Monday." There is a clip in his tone that I have heard before, the subject closed, and, for a moment, I don't see his bare body or the tight fit of the underwear. For a moment, I only see defeat.

I threaten Trey with eviction, and he finally puts on the robe, balking at the idea of lying down in the makeshift bed. "I'm not having you tuck me in," he complains. "I'm a grown man." He sits at the other end of the couch, stretching his legs out, his bare feet against the rug.

"I'm not tucking you in," I argue. "I'm just trying to get you to be comfortable."

"I'm not going to be comfortable lying down, covered in blankets, while you do laundry. It feels awkward."

I pause, mid-fold. Maybe now isn't the time to fold my towels. Maybe now is the time to excuse myself and let the man sleep. He is right. This should be awkward, only it doesn't feel that way to me. It feels, for the first time since I've met him, natural and relaxed. "I don't feel awkward," I say, completing the trifold action and neatly stacking the towel into the basket. "Hasn't anyone ever taken care of you? Just think of me as—"

"STOP." He holds up a hand. "You're about to ruin all of my future fantasies about you."

"Ha." I roll my eyes. "Little chance of that." I frown at him. "Besides, you aren't supposed to *have* fantasies about me, or anyone else at Marks. In case you missed the memo, the CEO is a real dick about fraternization." I smirk at the thought of his last all-company email, one that spanned three pages, all devoted to ensuring that our hands are kept to ourselves, and our minds are clear of the gutter. Which had been humorous, in a way, since the company is all about sex and seduction.

"You're confusing the rules. I'm allowed to have fantasies; I'm just not allowed to act on them." He crosses his arms over his chest and rests his head against the back of the couch, his eyes closing, as if he hasn't just delivered a baby of ridiculous proportions.

That's the problem with beautiful men. They don't know their impact; they don't realize how a casually tossed out thought can be devoured, obsessed over, life-changing. He's lucky that I've known men like him before, I've friended them, I understand the careless way they wield their looks, their flirtatious comments that mean nothing. He is on the verge of sleep, and there was less stock in that statement than there is energy in his body.

"Are you happy, Kate?" The question is mumbled, his eyes still closed.

I consider my answer, doing a quiet self-assessment of the key factors (love, health, quality of life = all acceptable). *Acceptable.* Does acceptability equal happiness? I think it does. I think, for a woman in her mid-thirties, happiness is more about the lack of negatives. And right now, my list of negatives is pretty short. "I am. Are you?"

He doesn't say anything. A full minute passes, then his hand falls limply from the couch arm, and the muscles in his face go slack.

I finish folding the laundry in silence, my mind still stuck on his question.

Am I happy?

Him

The touch on my shoulder is soft, then increasingly incessant—a press that is becoming more annoying then nurturing. It stops, then someone lifts my ankles and pulls slightly. I open my eyes and watch Kate Martin attempt to pull an end table underneath my feet. "What are you doing?" I say, and she jumps slightly, the room dark, most of her in the shadows.

"You need to lie down," she whispers.

I turn my head and look at the bed she made, the corner of a blanket turned back, ready for me. I move slowly, my feet filled with lead, my neck sore, and roll onto my back, the pillows unbelievably soft. She moves over me, her hair soft against my chest, a faint scent of perfume tickling the edges of my senses. She pulls a blanket over me, and I open my mouth to thank her, but I can't get the words out before everything fades away.

If this moment was lingerie, it'd be our Shameless Robe, soft and warm to the touch, the sort of thing that you pull on and never take off.

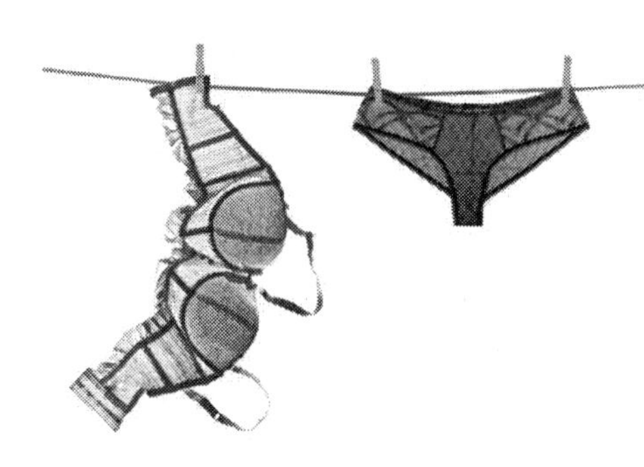

chapter 5
Her

"Of course you're happy." Mom pops pistachios in the seasoned manner of a competitive eater, her hands flying from the bowl to her mouth to the trash, all in perfect harmony. Around her neck, a neck massager purrs. "Why wouldn't you be happy?"

"You're not happy," Jess interjects, sitting in the chair next to Mom, her shoulders shuddering as the massage chair tortures her poor back fat to death. "No one who asks themselves that question is happy."

"Jess, are you happy?" Mom pauses, a pistachio shell before her lips, and peers at her youngest daughter.

"Meh." Jess mashes a button on the remote, and her feet slowly lift, her head tilting back. "This, though. This could make me happy. Kate, spend all of that money you're making and get me this for Christmas."

"She's not getting you a massaging chair for Christmas," Mom intones, her fingers digging into her purse and coming up with a fresh handful of nuts. "She's got to save her money for the wedding."

"Actually, I'm not getting you that chair because it's six thousand dollars," I say, leaning forward and looking at the black contraption currently surrounding my feet. "Did this thing hurt when you guys did it? I think it's broken. It's crushing my toes."

"That's normal," Mom says, with the air of a seasoned Brookstone shopper. "I think it wakes up your blood vessels or something like that."

"Excuse me?" We all turn to the man, a store employee who clutches a clipboard in one hand. "You can't eat in here."

"Sure I can." Mom defiantly stuffs two nuts past her coral-red lips. "John told me I could."

He sighs. "No one named John works here."

Jess meets my eyes, and I look at my feet to hide my smile. Poor guy.

"I didn't say John!" she says indignantly. "I said Jim. Or was it Jeff?" She waves a hand dismissively and a pistachio escapes, flying toward a display of drones. "Something like that. A tall guy." She sniffs. "With glasses."

"There's no eating in here," he repeats. "I'll have to ask you to leave."

"I've got thirteen minutes left," Jess pipes up, holding a remote almost the size of my head. "We can't le-le-leave-ve-ve yet-et-et-et." The last words of her sentence reverberate out of her, her chin shaking as the chair starts that sort of karate chopping motion that masseuses all love.

"Jacob *said* I could eat in here!" Mom insists, and I reach down and turn off the foot massager. Beside me, a little girl stops, her finger crawling up her right nostril as she stares at my mother. *Move along, little lady. Nothing to see here.* My mental urging has little effect. She plops down on the floor, and I meet Jess's eyes. *Let's go*, I mouth.

It is hard to tell, with all the shuddering of her body, but I think she nods.

"Does this make you happy?" Mom stands, and the cord rips out of the neck massager, the soothing purr gone. "Taking food out of little old ladies' mouths?" The man reaches for her arm, and she snatches it away, her cup full of pistachio shells swinging through the air, a rainfall of white half-moons cascading down.

My eyes catch the little girl's, and she grins, showing a few missing teeth.

"So anyway, as of last month, I'm banned from Brookstone." I reach over and turn on the heated seats, my elbow brushing against Trey's.

Craig, had I told him this story, which I did not, would have been appalled. Trey merely grins. "Any Brookstone? Or just the one in Fashion Square?"

I pause. "I'm not sure. Maybe just that one."

"So you're not fully a bad girl. Just in Westfield."

"Well… yes." I smile. "But again, that was all my mother's fault. I was completely innocent."

"I'd rather picture you as a rebel." He reaches forward and starts the navigation, the car informing us that a turn is approaching in fourteen miles. "Remind me again why we didn't fly to San Francisco."

"Quality time together," I say, reaching forward and pulling the water bottle from my bag. "Team building. The chance to see my excellent navigational skills."

"Money," he drawls.

"Are we saving money?" I squint, then shrug. "Oh, well. That too."

I pull off my heels and settle into the seat, tucking one foot underneath my butt. I pick up my cell phone, and look through my texts. According to Trey's recovered Tesla—in fine condition, minus one side mirror—we've got six hours to go, which includes a power charging break. And …. according to my schedule, we'll be fine on time. Tonight, dinner and drinks with suppliers. Tomorrow morning, I've got interviews with two different designers, then we'll make the trek back. I check for texts from Craig, but there are none. This trip is causing me to miss our second Mensa meeting. He seems as relieved as I am with the timing, one I carefully orchestrated. At our twenty-year anniversary, we'll laugh about it. But now, the bitch that is Mensa seems like an anchor tied to our relationship, sinking Craig's viewpoint of me and dragging my tolerance level down along with it.

I look over at Trey, who is relaxed against the seat, his eyes on the road, and flip through the list of questions I had jotted down to discuss during this drive. It had been Jess's idea, being convinced that—given six hours alone with me—we could become best friends and cement my job security forever. She doesn't understand fashion, the fickle beast that it is. She doesn't understand that my job security hinges on my performance, my ability to revitalize the Marks Lingerie brand. I can bond with Trey Marks until I'm blue in the face and it won't change the fact that his company is dying. I wet my lips. "How did you get into lingerie?"

It's a story that should be known, should be sprinkled over every article, Wikipedia page, and company bio. But I've found nothing online, no breadcrumb trail to explain how this man ended up with the sixth largest lingerie company in the world. Were the rumors right? Had he seduced an old woman out of her riches?

"It's a long story." He glances at me. "And fairly boring."

As if anything about him could be. I set down my phone. "I like boring stories. If it's really good, maybe you can lull me to sleep and not have to deal with my incessant chatter for the next six hours."

He gives a short smile—more polite than authentic. "Maybe another time."

I huff out a protest. "I can't properly create a vision if I don't know the bones of the company."

"Hasn't seemed to bother you so far." He shifts in his seat. "Besides, it's not in my job description."

"Ha. Funny." I reach down and dig into my purse. "Do you allow people to eat in your car?"

"Of course." He glances over, watching as I pull out a bag of M&Ms, ripping open the top and offering it to him. "No thanks."

"If you're not going to tell me, I'm just going to invent something scandalous and put it on the website. Poof." I shrug. "Done."

"I'm terrified," he says dryly.

"As you should be. Wait until everyone finds out that you were a homeless street performer, playing a ukulele outside a trim factory. You broke in one night, looking for food, and built a hammock bed out of straps and a ukulele bag out of lace. One day, a wealthy woman saw your ukulele bag and—"

"Please stop." He smiles, and it is an actual smile, one without sexual pull or cocky undertones. "You're offending street performers everywhere."

"That's not offensive," I say indignantly. "It's the start of a ukulele-playing mogul! Look what you became!" I gesture to him, and his smile widens.

"Please stop saying 'ukulele."

"I'll stop saying 'ukulele,' if you tell me the real story."

He rolls his eyes. "Fine." He puts both hands on the steering wheel. "I started at Bloomingdale's, in their ED program."

"How'd you get into that?" I interrupt him despite my best attempt to listen. South Central and Bloomingdale's … talk about two completely different worlds.

He grins. "When I was thirteen, I was caught at Bloomingdale's, shoplifting. The loss prevention manager wanted to know what a thirteen-year-old kid wanted with a woman's blouse."

"A girlfriend?" I guess.

He scowls. "No. My mother. She had an interview—for a real job, an assistant in a real estate firm—none of her clothes were appropriate." He falls silent and I remember. The stripper mother.

"That's sweet."

He chuckles. "It's not too sweet. I had lifted a few other items. Things for me, a thong for this girl I was dating. Anyway, the guy offered for me to work off the items in their stock room. I agreed, and we sort of became close." He glances over at me. "That guy was eventually promoted, to a high enough level that—when college didn't work out for me—he had the pull to offer me a job."

I stay quiet, trying to piece together the picture of a young Trey Marks, one who sounds like a street thug … with the polished man who sits beside me.

He shifts in the expensive seat, a bit of his cologne drifting over and teasing my senses. "You know Vicka Neece?"

Vicka Neece … the name is familiar, but takes a moment to place. "Sure. The Creative Director for Victoria's Secret." Maybe the rumor mill had it wrong. I lean forward.

"We used to work together at Bloomingdale's. There was a bit of a connection there."

A connection. I don't have to look up Vicka Neece to imagine what she looks like. Victoria's Secret doesn't hire ugly women. She and Trey probably just looked at each other and orgasmed. I wrestle out a peanut M&M with a little more aggression than is necessary. "And?"

I say brightly, and it doesn't sound fake at all.

"And then my father died," he says flatly, and I suddenly regret my mockery.

"I'm sorry," I say quietly.

"He didn't have much to his name, but he had taken out a five-million-dollar policy three months prior to his death. A bunch of Italians came after me for part of that. Vicka Neece was interested in the rest. She pitched me on opening a lingerie brand." He shrugs. "It wasn't that hard to talk me into. I was twenty-six. I was stupid."

His father. Something in my chest, a clog that hates the idea of Trey and an older woman, clears. "How were you stupid? You made it into a real player. I mean, right now we're struggling, but—"

"I don't regret opening the company. I regret losing Vicka. We were successful when she was here, when she was in control. And we sailed on her vision for the first few years after she left. But then, everything started to fall to shit." He glances at me. "I don't have to tell you that you are the sixth Creative Director we've had in five years."

No, he didn't have to tell me that. I had all of their files in the cabinet in my office. I had reviewed all of their work, all of their visions. Vicka Neece hadn't had a file in that stack. Whatever her history with Trey, it had been erased before I got there.

"Did you ever try to get her back?" It's almost a waste of a question, her job at VS putting her on the top rung of every fashion hierarchy. If I ever got that job, I'd be there until I died, or until I was forcibly carried out.

"No." He rubs his neck. "We had opened the company as friends. A few months in, we started fucking."

The words are so rough that I wince. "Just fucking?"

"I don't know. It got so that I couldn't tell the company from her, or our relationship from sex. I got jealous, she got jealous. We started fucking less and fighting more. And then she was gone. Packed up her office in the middle of the night and moved back to New York."

"Do you still talk to her?"

"Fashion's a small world. We see each other sometimes, but not much is said. I'm pissed at her for leaving; she's pissed at me and I'm not even sure why. If you ask her now about Marks Lingerie, she won't even admit that she worked here."

Ouch. I take another M&M, this one gentler in its retrieval.

"Truth be told…" he glances over at me. "I'm glad you are engaged. It makes everything easier."

I crunch down on the chocolate-covered candy and my jaw pops in response. My mind tries to process that statement, but draws a blank.

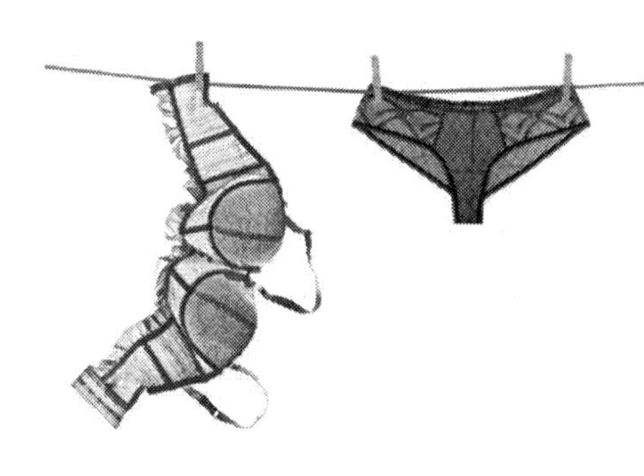

chapter 6
Him

I have grossly underestimated this woman. I stare down at the current sketch, a dark bustier with leather and lace accents. I flip the page and see the exact same cut, same style, but pale pink and white, with delicate cording instead of leather, and petite diamonds instead of silver studs. It's a naughty and nice collection, two separate lines that will battle each other on store racks, the naughty collection a bit dominating in colors and trimmings, the nice designs almost virginal. It isn't a new concept, but the brilliance is in the actual designs. "Our team designed these?"

"Yes." She reaches forward, and I brush her hand away.

"Just let me look for a moment." It's too big of an undertaking. I flip through a stack of designs and try to count them. In four months, she's orchestrated forty, maybe fifty, designs? "How many of these have been actually produced and fitted?"

"Fourteen."

A more bearable number, but still. I think of production costs, of inventory levels. If it sells, if it sells well … a new set of problems. Cash flow. Production levels. I feel a knot of anxiety grip my chest.

"It's good." She sounds irritated, and I look up to see her arms crossed tightly over her chest. "I know it's a different style than your last few years, but—"

"I agree. I love it." I set down the page and sit back in my chair. "Sit down, please. You're stressing me out."

For the first time in months, she doesn't talk back. She obeys. Something in the submission stirs at me, my mind losing focus for a brief moment. I close my eyes and return to the issue at hand. "It's a big investment. Right now … it's a tough swing."

"It will be even harder next quarter," she says quietly. "We need to fix things now. Immediately."

She's right, and I know it. My fear is that her fix, these pieces … if I invest in them, if I take that leap, it will be Marks Lingerie's last. After this, there are no more favors to beg or pockets to pick.

"Let me show it to the sales team." I meet her eyes. "If they like it, then let's do it."

"Do what? The fourteen pieces?" She stands and steps forward.

"Whatever you want, as long as you can back the product up with cost margins and deliverability." I reach out and touch her hand, stopping her from picking up the presentations. She looks at me, and I choose my next words carefully. "I'm wagering everything on this. On *you.* I need you to understand how important it is for this to succeed."

She nods, and in her eyes I see the confidence I once had. The reckless belief that, no matter what, I would succeed. When did I lose that fire? When did I become convinced I would fail?

She turns to leave, and without her, the room feels dead.

Her

Black strips of latex cut across spandex. A collar with a front ring, back buckle. Hidden underwire that makes the sample-sized model look magnificently large-breasted. In any other setting, it should be trashy. But with the right lines, cuts, and support, it is sophisticatedly beautiful.

Six months into this job, and I fight the urge to jump up and down like a school girl.

"It's uncomfortable." The model punctures my elation with two simple words.

"How uncomfortable?" I glance down at Vern, the technical designer, who looks at the model.

"Pretty bad." She tilts her head, then turns it. "The worst is the collar-thing. It's itchy."

"On the edges or the backing?" Vern stands and moves behind her.

"The edges."

"What else is uncomfortable?" I look down at the fitting schedule, cursing to myself. We are behind schedule, not just for today, but for this month. I shot for twenty-two new pieces, and I'm kicking myself in the ass for it. Something that seemed possible two months ago turned difficult one month ago, and now appears to be pretty-fucking-impossible. I glance back at the model and fight the urge to scream at her to hurry up. Maybe this is why Claudia was such a bitch. I am just six months into this role, and I can already feel the fraying of human qualities.

"It feels like it's cutting into my rib cage. The boning."

"Okay. Move around for me and tell me when the pain increases or decreases."

"Pain?" I interrupt Vern. "Or discomfort?"

The model stiffens, her lips parting, eyes widening, and I growl without looking over my shoulder. "You aren't supposed to be here."

From behind me, he chuckles. "You didn't think I'd let you have all of the fun, did you?"

I turn, and, from my place on the stool, we are eye level. "Fittings aren't fun. No one thinks fittings are fun."

"I like fittings," the model breathes, and she suddenly doesn't look uncomfortable at all. Trey's eyes don't move to her; they stay on me. I thought he was beautiful from my spot on the ground. At this elevated level, he's even more devastating.

I hop down from the stool before I lose all intelligence. "What do you think?" I nod to the woman.

"It's gorgeous." He walks around her slowly.

"Right. It looks great, but she's saying it's uncomfortable."

"I can manage. It's not that bad," she offers.

Vern mumbles something under his breath, and Trey chuckles in response. "Uh-uh." I shake my head at them. "Stop that shit." I push at Trey's shoulder, then point to the door. "And you, go crunch numbers somewhere. I've got a dozen more of these to work through." I flip over the page. "Vern, you got this? I'm going to move on to Cecile's model."

"I'll leave in a minute. Let me borrow you for a second."

I look up from the page. "Now?" I shake my head. "No. I'm going to keep these guys here 'til midnight at this rate. Whatever it is, shoot me an email or show me in the morning." I can't deal with any more problems, or decisions, or his need for an opinion on the interior pages of the spring catalog.

"I'm borrowing Kate," he calls out. "Everyone, take five."

"No one take five," I yell. "Everyone keep working." He pulls at my arm and successfully manages to drag me toward the door. I half-heartedly struggle until we are in the hall, the door closed. "What?" I beg. "I've seriously got so much to do."

"I just got off the phone with Paris."

"And?" I grip his arm.

"They doubled their last order. They loved your designs."

I shriek, throwing my arms around his neck, my clipboard catching him on the side of his face. I apologize as I grip him tightly, jumping up and down. When I release him, he rubs the side of his face with a wince. "Sorry," I breathe. "I'm just so happy!"

"Are we able to deliver?"

"Yes," I say quickly. "I think so." I nod, my fingers drumming excitedly over the clipboard. "If you stop interrupting fittings and turning my models' brains to mush."

He chuckles and steps back. "I'll let you do your thing. I've got more pitches to make."

I smile and hold his gaze. It's his victory in sales, and mine in design. And this moment, this baby moment of joy before the panic returns, is the best in my career so far.

"They doubled their last order. They loved your designs."

Marks Lingerie is on its way back.

The Honor Bar in Beverly Hills. We steal two spots in the corner, my purse hanging off the back of the chair, his jacket taken off, and order dinner. I ignore my diet and get a cheeseburger. He orders the same, then adds two Coronas.

I make a face. "I can't drink tonight." I pull at the clip, loosening my hair. My scalp burns, and I run my fingers through my roots, massaging the skin.

"Why not? We're done for today. I'll have your car brought to your house." He smiles, and pushes the tabletop candle to the side. "I think you need a night to relax."

"I'm relaxed." I lean against the wall and close my eyes.

"You're exhausted. There's a difference."

I am exhausted. Half of me is dying for my bed, my quiet apartment, my ability to sleep in late tomorrow. The other half of me feels like celebrating. It was that half of me that accepted his dinner invite.

"Why don't you call Craig? See if he can join us."

The waiter returns, beers in hand, and I watch him set down the bottles. "He can't," I reply. "He has a Chemistry Association meeting tonight. It's a monthly thing." I smile. "Exciting stuff."

"Sounds like it." He lifts his beer. "Cheers."

I lift my bottle. "Just one drink," I say. "I can't be out too late."

"Sure." He shrugs. "You're the boss."

I smile at the joke, and take a sip.

I lean forward. "So I walk into the room and they are both standing there, naked." I giggle, a hiccup forcing its way out. "I thought they were gay. And I started to apologize, you know, for interrupting them—"

"You started to apologize to your boyfriend?" Trey leans forward, a confused look on his face.

"Yes," I wince. "It was right when there was all this PC stuff about accepting homosexuality, and all I could think was that I wanted him to know that it was okay—you know—him being gay."

"I don't understand where this story is going."

I lower my voice and lean in. "They weren't gay. They were…" I glance to the table beside us to make sure they aren't listening. "They were waiting for *me*." He doesn't respond and I sigh, forced to fully explain it. "They wanted to have sex with me. Together!" I take a sip of the beer. "It's called a threesome."

The corner of his mouth lifts into a smirk. "Oh yes. I'm familiar with the term."

Of course he is. He's probably had one. Or two. Or five. I move past his smirk and on with my story. "So anyway … that was my first boyfriend. A terrible candidate to lose my virginity to."

"Wait." He holds up a palm. "You just skipped over all of the good stuff." He sits back in his chair and lifts his beer. "Did you enjoy it?"

"Enjoy what?" I eye my now-empty beer, and try to calculate how many I've had. Three? Four? The waiter swings by and delivers two more.

"The threesome."

"Ew!" I make a face. "Seriously? You think I did that?"

He studies my face carefully, then shrugs, his broad shoulders lifting the crisp white shirt. "I guess not." He sounds almost disappointed.

"Why would I?" I press, and now I'm getting irritated. "Do you know how offensive that is? Two guys taking turns on me? Using me? I didn't even *know* the other guy. "

"Easy, Kate." He pushes aside his old beer and reaches for the new one. "I was just asking for the story."

"The story is that I left. And I don't know what they did amongst themselves." I make a face, then realize my voice may have gotten a little too loud in my indignation. "Sorry for yelling," I whisper loudly.

"It's okay," he whispers back.

I pick up a spoon and stab at the brownie, a desert from an hour ago, one that has been stabbed to death by my occasional tastings. It *is* okay. It's more than okay. It's normal. Normal people think that threesomes are gross. Craig would definitely think that threesomes are gross. I've never even told him that story for fear that he would judge me out of mere proximity to the act.

"So…" Trey drawls. "You don't like threesomes. Anything else I should know about you?"

I glance up and meet his eyes, and with just a flash of that smile, we are back to normal.

The lights of Torrance are blurring, the taxi bumping along the street, and I watch two bums argue in the brief moment before we pass. "It's the next right," I call out.

Trey checks his phone. "God, I can't believe it's almost midnight."

"Normally in bed by this time?" I tease.

"Normally in someone's bed by this time." He grins at me, a playful one, and I groan in response.

"You didn't have to escort me home. I'm a big girl. I could have gotten my own ride."

"I would have worried. This way I can properly see you to your door and earn gentleman points in the process." He looks out the window. "No offense, Kate, but we have to get you out of this neighborhood."

I reach down and grab my purse, the car slowing down before my building. "This neighborhood is fine. But if you want to give me a raise…" I shrug. "I won't fight you on it."

"Stay here. I'll get your door." He gets out, and I wait, watching as he approaches my door and opens it with a grand flourish. "M'lady."

I laugh, stepping from the cab and over the broken sidewalk. Before me, my building looms, and I have a moment of drunk appreciation for my first floor unit. He tells the cabbie to wait and walks me to the door, pausing before it, his face growing serious. "Monday, let's talk about a raise."

"Wow. You really are drunk." I pull out my keys and flip through them.

"No, I'm serious." He meets my eyes. "I'll give you anything you want."

He meant an increase in salary, but it came out wrong, his voice too husky, his body too close. I step back, but our gaze holds, and I almost change direction, lean in, reach out. He clears his throat, and the moment breaks. I look down, and manage to fit the key in the building's front door.

"Thanks for seeing me to the door." The words squeak a little on their way out. "I'll be fine from here."

He steps back, and the darkness of the walkway obscures his face. "Have a good night, Kate." He pauses, his hands sliding into his pockets. Behind him, the cab exhaust smokes in the night air. "See you tomorrow."

I give a little wave and escape inside, my heart beating, hands trembling as I flip the deadbolt over.

"I'll give you anything you want."

In that moment, it wasn't a raise I wanted.

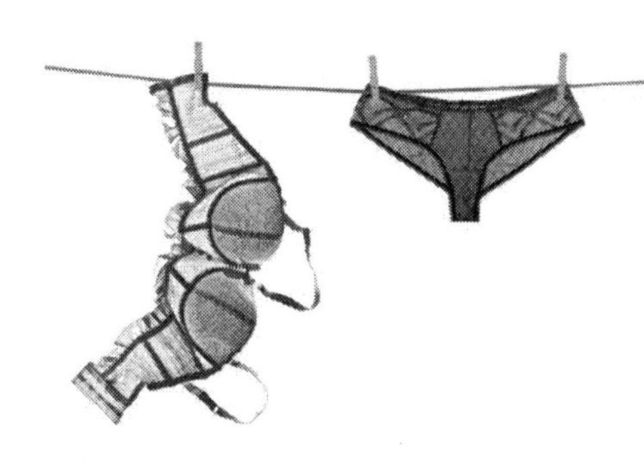

chapter 7
Her

"You're packing it wrong." Craig stands next to me, his hand on his hips, his head shaking.

"It's fine." I shut the suitcase lid and lean on it, struggling with the zipper.

"Kate, stop." He bats at my hand. "We need to pull everything out and repack. You don't need so many clothes."

"What I don't need is you telling me how to pack. Go in the living room," I say crossly. "Let me zip this up." I push on his shoulder and watch as he steps back, a pained look in his eyes. It's cruel to not let him pack, to not let him use his T shirt folding board to ensure that all of the edges are crisp and similarly sized. But letting him pack would mean that he'd see the red lace lingerie that I tucked inside, a new Marks item that hasn't even rolled off to stores yet. I'd like to keep it a surprise, something to pull out on Saturday night, in celebration of my birthday.

I get the suitcase closed, the zipper straining but holding, and I lug it into the living room, giving a ta-da! motion that goes completely ignored by Craig, who zeros in on each of my suitcase's wheels, examining and then lubricating them, using a tiny squeeze bottle that he returns to a Ziploc bag upon completion. "Ready?" I say dryly, glancing at my watch. It doesn't matter if he isn't. We've got a good five hours until the flight. There is no Earthly reason why we would leave the house now, except that Craig doesn't like to leave anything to chance. I thought he overdid it when we went to San Diego for the night. It turns out that international travel puts him on a whole new plane of neurotics. I eye Craig and wonder if I'm making a mistake bringing him. This is a work event after all, a shopping trip to purchase leftover inventory from an old undergarments factory. Our four-day trip, if the inventory is quality, could save us a few hundred thousand dollars. In my initial mention of the trip to Craig, I could have just left it at that. Instead, fueled by wine and a $200 scratch-off ticket win, I'd invited him along.

"I'm ready." He tests out the wheels, rolling the suitcase in a quick circle. "I've got our itinerary and travel documents in the car already. Let's go."

I smile and loop my arm through his. "I'm excited."

He returns the smile, leaning forward and giving me a quick peck on the lips. "Me too, sweetie."

"Bon voyage!" I cheer, throwing my arms into the air.

"Allons-y," he corrects. "Bon Voyage is wishing someone else a good trip."

"Sure. Whatever." I grab the handle of my suitcase and skip toward the door.

Hong Kong is both everything I expected and like nothing I could have imagined. I stand in the middle of a busy street and lift my arms, spinning in the crowd, the neon lights everywhere, the air full of foreign smells and sounds, the clatter of languages like a comforting blanket of anonymity. I catch Trey's eyes and wave, the corner of his mouth pulling up in response, his eyes dropping back to the cash in his hand, his discussion with the street vendor continuing, a back and forth negotiation about scooter rentals, a conversation that Craig is panicking over, his repeated attempts to get my attention ignored. "Relaaaxxxx," I call out to him. He doesn't trust Trey; that is the problem. He hasn't learned the carefree ease with which Trey manages to handle things. It's been nine months, and I'm just now learning to leap when he offers his hand. Because that's how he is. He doesn't ask you to risk, unless he is taking that journey alongside you. If I fail, he fails. And if a street peddler in the biggest city in the world screws Craig over, he's screwing over Trey Marks also. And that scenario is as unlikely as, well … a tiny speck of moisture hits my cheek and I look up in delight, a kaleidoscope of white flurries drifting down. I jerk forward, waving my hands in big circles to get their attention. "Guys! It's SNOWING!"

Trey stands, and Craig and I watch as he lifts his glass toward us. "A toast," he announces, that trademark grin pulling at the edge of his mouth.

I glance down at my own wineglass, surprised to find it half empty. Hadn't he just topped me off … what, five minutes ago? Or ten? It was when we'd been telling Craig that story—the one about Marie from Accounting, and her Halloween costume. I giggle, and lift my glass. We should drink more. We should travel more. With my latest raise, and Craig's … well, Craig never spends any money so he should have mountains of it — there is no reason why we don't have more fun. Like this. Halfway across the world, in a place where foreign languages bounce off exotic walls, and we are eating fried silkworms for God's sake. Why, in three years together, are we just doing this *now*?

Trey clears his throat, and looks at me in an almost stern fashion. "Kate, I do believe that you are drunk."

I giggle again, a completely uncharacteristic act, and stop myself, analyzing my alcohol consumption and present mood. I *am* drunk. I feel almost proud at the fact, and that itself is even *further* testimony to the fact that I *must* be drunk. I, Kate Martin, eternal good girl and dotter of all I's, am officially drunk. In Hong Kong. With two of the best guys—

"She's about to cry," Craig blurts out, looking at Trey with concern.

I sniff. I can't help it. They are so different. Craig is so good to me. And he tries so hard to be the best partner; he's going to be a wonderful father, and he's suuuuch a good person on the inside. And then you have Trey, who is, like, this perfect sexy unicorn—not that he has a horn sticking out of his head or anything like that—he's just so … I close my eyes and try to find the right word, the one that embodies how special and unique he is. How he can make my day by just smiling. Like how, right now, he is looking at me, in the kindest, sweetest way, as if—

"DON'T CRY," Craig says, very loudly, his face close to mine, my nose catching a whiff of the tuna tartare he had for an appetizer.

"OKAY," I say back, just as loudly and exaggerated as he had, as if being drunk made me deaf in some way. "I WILL NOT CRY."

My eyes meet with Trey's, and he winks.

2 AM. My buzz peaks, then falls, my joy ebbing into something else, something dark and contemplative, where all of my thoughts bubble to the surface and demand to be examined. Craig and I step into the elevator, and I watch the floor numbers rise.

I think there is something fundamentally wrong with my relationship.

In three years of dating, we haven't had a single fight. In three years, we have fit together easily, me overlooking any imperfections, and hiding any qualities that I thought he wouldn't approve of. I love him, but I've never been passionate about him; I've never obsessed over him. Shouldn't a woman, at some point, obsess over the man she is going to spend the rest of her life with? Once, when I was looking up an email on Craig's phone, I had the momentary idea to check his text messages, to see who he was communicating with, and what was being said. I hadn't, the idea preposterous that Craig would be cheating on me, or flirting with someone else. A waitress once hit on him, and he got so worked up about it that he made the poor waitress sit down and listen to him explain the history of our relationship. We stopped going to that restaurant, just to avoid another uncomfortable interaction with her.

Our hotel room is dark, no lights left on, the curtains drawn. I open the top drawer of the dresser, moving aside my sweater and consider the lingerie set hidden underneath it. I replace the sweater and sit on the bed, listening to Craig brush his teeth, then floss. When he comes into the room and unzips his pants, I watch him remove them, hanging them neatly back on the hanger, his body slowly unwrapped as he removes his shirt and follows the same process. His body is the perfect specimen for a doctor's office: well-exercised, no flab, but only moderate muscle tone, nothing bulky enough to stress the heart. He comes to me naked, gently pulling me to my feet and we kiss, his tongue tasting of wintergreen, his skin cool beneath my fingers. He pulls at the zipper of my dress and I help him. He goes to his knees, and I lie back on the bed, one leg over his shoulder, his mouth gentle against me, and I dig my fingers into his hair when I come.

I think it's the alcohol that has numbed me. There is no reason, when he moves to the bed and pushes inside of me, that I don't emotionally react. No reason why, when we finish and I roll over in bed, my dress still on, hair still up, that I should feel alone.

But I do. I lay my hand across the dark grey sheets, the diamond glinting at me, and I feel the deep certainty that I am making a mistake.

At 4 AM, I wake up Craig and tell him everything.

Him

I end the call and nod to the waiter, waiting for him to replace my drink. I eye the third place setting, and regret, for the hundredth time, allowing her to bring her fiancé along. Initially, I had thought it a good idea. I thought that seeing her happy, seeing her future—it might make everything between her and I a little clearer, a little less tempting. That plan backfired as soon as they arrived. This guy isn't right for her. Hell, he's completely wrong for her. But I can't tell her that. If I do, she'll dismiss it, and then there will be animosity, and as close as we've become during the past nine months, I'm not certain we can bury that conversation and move on.

I run a finger over the tines of my fork, pushing down on the silver, irritated by the fact that he is here, putting a damper on everything. Today, we should be celebrating, the merchandise purchase complete, a chunk of money saved, everything continuing to move toward success. Instead, I'll be staring across the table at him, and pairing all of the ways he is wrong for her against all of his strengths.

Unfortunately, he does have a few strengths.
He's attractive, in a Brooks Brothers, men's catalogue sort of way. Perfectly neat hair, straight teeth, boyish good looks.
He's successful, assuming she's happy as middle-class.
He's smart, annoyingly so, something he has gone out of his way to point out.

He also seems oblivious to the fact that I want to fuck his future wife. He seems to have no concern over our long hours, or casual familiarity, or the moments that our eyes meet across the table, wordless communication in just the tiny movements of a smile or glance.

He shouldn't be this calm, or this friendly. He should be questioning our friendship, and subtly asserting his dominance. There should be a healthy distance between us, a squaring off of masculinity, a rolling up of sleeves in the fight over this woman. My woman.

That is how all of this should play out. That is the game I know how to fight.

I can't fight a nice, well-mannered pushover. It would make me look like an ass. It would push her away.

I reach for my glass and mentally correct myself. It doesn't matter how he reacts, or how the game should be played. I can't fight him because I shouldn't have her. It's the mantra I keep forgetting, the plan that keeps going astray.

The restaurant door opens, and I know it's her from the smile on the maître d's face.

 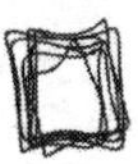 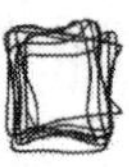

"Where's Craig?" I pull out her chair, glancing toward the front of the restaurant. It's terrible, but a part of me hopes that he is sick, some sort of stomach bug that will keep him in their room and out of our hair for the next two days.

"Something came up, late last night. He's on the way to the airport now. He has to go home." She picks up the napkin and spreads it in her lap, her eyes on the motion. Something is wrong, her voice too forcibly light.

I sit down and smooth my own napkin, keeping my gaze on her. "Do you need to go with him? I can handle the rest of the meetings without you."

"No." The shake of her head is short and quick, almost a shudder.

"It's fine. I'll see him when I get back." She smiles at me, and something is definitely wrong, the lines of her face pulling at the wrong places, her eyes avoiding mine, her study of the menu uncharacteristically focused.

I fight a war between protective aggression and giving her space, my tongue poised, unsure of how to act. I catch her eyes and there is a flash of raw vulnerability, silently begging me to leave it alone. I reach forward, passing her the basket of bread, and eye the ring that still sits on her finger. "So, no Craig."

"No."

"And our meeting with the factory rep is at ten?"

"Yes."

"I hope you use bigger words in our meeting. You're the only chance we have to sound intelligent."

The corner of her mouth twitches, and it feels like a monumental victory. "Okay."

"And you know you've piled a lot of extra work on me."

Her eyebrow raises, and a hint of life enters her eyes. "In what way?"

I let out a heavy sigh. "Now I've got to entertain you for the next two days. Play host, get you drunk on Hong Kong sake, and give you a vacation you'll never forget."

She rolls her eyes and picks up the menu. "Shut up. We both know I'll be getting room service tonight, and you'll be banging some Chinese whore."

"I'm *canceling* the Chinese whore," I say with a hurt tone. "I mean, I *was* going to bang her, but you and your inconvenient loneliness just cost her the greatest orgasms of her life."

"Oh my God." She lifts the menu higher to hide her smile. "Please stop."

Her foot bumps against my leg, and I look at my own menu, wishing that ring was off her finger and this restaurant was deserted.

Her

"I'm not drinking that!" I call up to Trey, hoping he can read lips because the noise in the club is deafening. He smiles down at me and I tug on his dress pants, smacking a hand across the top of his shoe to get his attention.

Standing on top of the bar, he calls out something and the crowd erupts into cheers, a chant starting which I can't understand. I raise my hands in question and he points to the girl next to me, yelling something at her. The girl, a pig-tailed sexpot with cat eyes and combat boots, leans forward and presses her mouth to the ice block, her eyes flicking up to Trey. He tilts a bottle and red liquor flows down a gulley, through the ice and into her mouth. It looks unsanitary and extremely sexual, two directions I have no plans of stumbling down tonight. She closes her eyes and swallows, lifting her mouth from the ice and wiping across her lips with the back of the hand. She gestures me forward.

"No!" I wave my hands at Trey, shaking my head emphatically, but the crowd chants louder, fists pounding the bar top, bodies beginning to jump in concert. He winces, as if he is innocent in all of this, then holds up one finger.

"One shot," he yells. "Just one!"

I can't. If I do this, if I yield to him, he will be hell. It will be like giving the devil keys to my kingdom. He will know that if he flashes me that smile, and gives me that wink, that I will bend, will behave, will do whatever he wants me to do. And I do mean *whatever*. His eyes catch mine and he crouches, smoothly setting down the liquor and swinging off the bar, landing beside me, his hand cupping the back of my waist and pulling me against him. He lowers his mouth to my ear. “Just one, Kate. For me.”

Maybe it is the proximity to him, or the way his voice softens on the last two words. Maybe it is the fact that I have to turn away from him and take that shot or I'll tilt my chin up and kiss him. Whatever the reason, I step away and up to the ice.

I tell myself that ice is sterile, and it doesn't matter that I'm putting my mouth in the same place where a stranger's was.
I tell myself that because I didn't tell Trey that I broke up with Craig. It makes this night fine, removes any romantic layers, and drinking with my boss is as inappropriate as this will get.
I close my eyes and wait for the alcohol, and tell myself that I don't care if I look sexy, or if Trey is proud of me, or impressed, or anything else.
The liquor hits my tongue and it's ice cold. I swallow it and stand, some leaking from the side of my mouth. As I go to clean it, Trey's hand is there, his fingers soft against my chin, and our eyes meet as he wipes away the liquor and then moves his hand up, gently sucking the edge of his thumb into his mouth.

Good Lord. This man will be the death of me.

My flight to Hong Kong had been bearable, Craig and I lucky enough to be seated next to one of those scrawny teenagers who wears headphones and doesn't hog the armrest. But flying back, Trey upgrades me to first class, an expensive transition I initially balk at. The mid-flight neck massage, private television, and sushi softens my resistance. The full bed, privacy curtain, and seven-hour nap have me swearing off coach forever.

“Is everything okay with Craig?”

I consider the question without turning to look at him. “He's fine. It was a work emergency. I think he's handled it." It'd be easy to tell him the truth; I should tell him the truth. Trey isn't just my boss—we have become friends. It'd be weird not to tell him.

But telling him I've broken off my engagement will lead to questions, ones that I haven't quite worked out in my head. Maybe, back in the US, I will change my mind. Maybe, after cataloguing all of the decision-making factors, I'll realize that I shouldn't have made such a life-altering decision while drinking. Maybe I'll call Craig and tell him that I'd made a mistake.

Or maybe I won't. I feel absolutely zero regret over my decision. If anything, I feel better—the knot of anxiety over our future gone, my possibilities wide open. Last night, I had the best night of my life. At some point, we had danced, in a dark club off a side street, one where drag queens greeted us at the door and disco pumped through the speakers. I've never danced. Not in college, definitely not in grad school. The formal events that Craig and I sometimes attended had a few slow songs we'd swayed to, in the most dignified manner possible. But nothing like last night. That had been arms up, ass shaking, gyrations. We had moved deep into the crowd, in a place of rough, jam-packed movement, his arms protectively wrapping around me, my body occasionally brushing against his to the tune of the techno. When we made it to the upstairs bar, we took tequila shots and found a jukebox. I put on a country song, managed to mix it with an Irish jig, and Trey laughed and told me that I was a terrible dancer. He also, over tapas in another bar, brushed my hair out of my face and told me that I was brilliant. I don't remember my response. I don't remember much of the rest of the evening, except that I fell asleep in a taxi, and he ended up carrying me to my room.

"Is it bad that I'm almost happy he went home early?" He leans his head back against the headrest and turns to smile at me. "I mean, I'm sure it ruined your birthday but—"

"It's not bad." I gave him a half-hearted smile. "I think it was a good coworker bonding experience." I reach out my glass, determined to return us to our proper relationship. "To Marks Lingerie."

His tongue runs along the inside of his bottom lip and he, almost reluctantly, lifts up his own glass. "To Marks. And to bonding with coworkers."

I tip back my glass and look away.

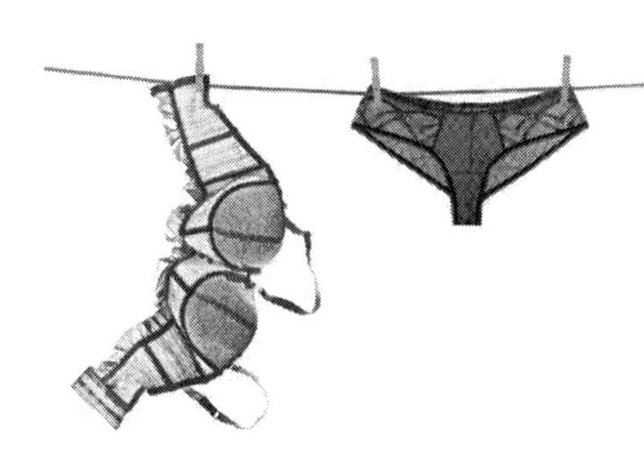

chapter 8
Her

"I just don't understand why you haven't told Trey." Jess pushes the shopping cart forward and stops beside a rack of purses, picking up a knock-off Betsey Johnson clutch. "It's been a month since you and Craig broke up. What do you guys talk about all the time?"

"Business." I spin a rack of sunglasses and pluck a pair off the top. "And other stuff. I don't know. He doesn't bring up Craig."

"You guys are weird." She holds up the clutch. "Do you think this is worth forty bucks?"

"No." I push the glasses on my face and bend down, looking into the mirror. "We aren't weird."

"You're totally weird. Even Mom thinks you're weird, so that's pretty much the kiss of death."

"In what way are we weird?" The glasses don't look terrible on me. I tilt my head, considering them.

"It's the way you look at each other. Like you guys are having subliminal conversations. It's rude, you know. When other people are there. I felt left out having lunch with the two of you. Plus, there's the whole attraction thing."

I take off the sunglasses and check the price tag, sighing as I return them to the rack. "Lots of friends are attracted to each other."

"Ummm … no." She tosses the clutch onto the pile and pushes the cart forward. "Actually, they aren't. It never works out."

"You liked Gabe Jordan."

"That was ninth grade, Kate." She checks her watch. "Shit. It's already two. We need to hurry."

I watch as she turns down a housewares aisle, her steps increasing in speed as she moves past the cooking items, bee-lining for a display of picture frames. Maybe Trey and I are weird. I certainly feel ungrounded at times, as if we are tip-toeing closer and closer to the line of inappropriateness. It's the reason I haven't told him about Craig. I feel like my fake relationship with him is a layer of protection, something to point to and say *See? We are just friends. We must be, since I am happily engaged.*

"Hasn't he asked about your ring?" Jess asks, carefully placing a picture frame into the cart.

"I told him I need to get it resized." A terrible excuse, but one he hadn't questioned.

"I still can't believe how smoothly your break-up went." She pauses. "Actually, never mind. I can. If I ever divorce Adam, I'm having Craig handle the entire thing."

She is right. My break-up with Craig couldn't have been more peaceful. He hadn't argued or shouted. There had been no tears or debates. He had listened to my fumbling attempt at discussing my feelings, then had moved to the closet and packed his bag. Before stepping out of the hotel room, we'd discussed our relationship going forward (cordial acquaintances), and whether he should contribute to the hotel bill (no). I have no doubt that, in his perfectly-organized home office, there had been an In Case We Break Up folder, complete with a list of to-do items. By the time I'd returned to the US, I had a box on my kitchen counter with all of my things from his house, along with a typed list of items he was requesting from me. He had paper-clipped a counselor's business card to the top of the list, along with signed papers from the bank that removed his name from all of our joint accounts. I'd returned his things the next week, and hadn't heard from him since.

I lean against the wall. "I'm worried telling Trey will change our relationship."

She looks at me. "That might not be a bad thing. He's ridiculously hot … you need a new man…" She shrugs as if my problems are solved.

"It's not that simple. Maybe if we were just friends—" I rub my eyes. "But the company needs us both. And he knows that. I don't think he'd even do anything with me, for fear of messing up that."

"Okay…" she drawls out, nodding at a passerby and moving farther down the aisle. "You're not making any sense. Do you want to date the guy or not?"

Do I *want* to date Trey? It isn't even worth considering. I *can't* date Trey. "No," I manage to say.

"No?" She raises her eyebrows in the knowing way that only a sister can.

"No," I repeat, and this time the short word is heavy with resolve.

She only laughs in response.

Him

The brunette is a younger version of Kate, her breasts swelling over the top of the balconet bra. I watch as she lounges against the pillows, one knee pulling up, a hip curving. A man in a suit steps forward, stopping before her.

"What do you think?" Kate asks quietly. Bulbs flash and there is a snap of the shutter.

"It's a gamble." I shrug. "But I like to gamble." *Like father, like son.*

"Think it'll be too risqué for the stores?" The man kneels before the model, his hand on her thigh.

"I'm not sure. But marketing loves the idea of sexualizing the shoot. They think they can get the photos to go viral." I pull out my phone and refresh my email.

"Still waiting on the Neiman Marcus order?"

"Yep." We are already solidly in the black for this season. However, their national order could give us firm footing to launch proper advertising. I lock the phone and slide it into my pocket.

"By the way…" she shifts in her heels, and I look over, something in her delivery giving me pause. "Craig and I broke up."

It is so unexpected that I take a step back, my heart doing a confused jig—made of elation and dread. I swallow. "Really."

"Yeah. I just thought you should know." She looks down at her clipboard, making a mark on the page. "Not that it changes anything. I just—"

"Why did you break up?" She had to have ended it. There was no way that he—that any man—would walk away from her.

"I don't know." Her shoulders lift. "I just felt that I might be making a mistake. And our relationship felt…" she pauses, and I feel my entire soul hang on the end of that sentence.

"…like a business relationship," she finally concludes. I understand what she is saying, the sterile way they had interacted, Craig's formal planning and execution of every task—but still. The word choice stabs at me.

I force myself to step closer to Kate, to return to our prior positions, my eyes on the models, the man now leaning over the woman, pinning her wrists to the bed. Kate tucks her hair behind her ear, and I catch a whiff of her perfume. She slides a hand down the shooting schedule, and I watch the delicate slide of her fingers across the page. She's single. My Kate is single. No ring on her finger, no calls on her phone, nothing to stop me from hooking my hand around her waist and pulling her against me. I turn and step away, call out to a photographer's assistant, and have him walk me through the lighting.

Working with her for the ten months—it has already been a strain on my willpower. Now, with Craig removed from the equation, will I be able to control myself? I glance back at her, my gaze moving up her body, enjoying the feminine curves, the casual slouch, the confident way she calls out to the photographer.

In my pocket, my phone vibrates, and I pull out the device, my heartbeat quickening at the email notification that appears. Neiman. The timing is suspect, and I glance up to the ceiling, wondering if the big man upstairs is trying to send me a message.

I open the email, and scroll quickly through the order, a smile pulling at my mouth as I see the purchase numbers. I stride over to her and wrap my arms around her, my chest to her back, my chin on her shoulder, my phone held out before her.

"Look," I whisper, and I fight the urge to gather her against me, to press my hips forward, against her body, to feel the curve of that ass against me. "Look what you did."

She twists around, throwing her arms around my neck, hugging it tightly. "*We* did," she states, and when she pulls away, she is beaming.

She's right. We did it. And dammit, I can't mess everything up now.

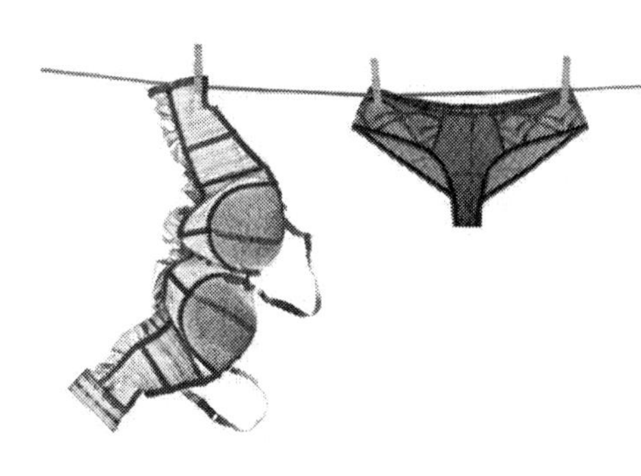

chapter 9
Her

four months later

Las Vegas. I win three thousand dollars on a slot machine and am stretched out on my bed, basking in my newfound riches, when Trey walks in. He cocks a brow at me and holds out his wrist. "I need help. This cufflink is a bitch."

I roll over and sit upright on the edge of the bed. When he steps forward, between my legs, I look up at him.

"This could get interesting," he murmurs, a wicked gleam in his eyes. His shoes settle into place, and his pant legs brush against the inside of my knees.

It won't. The man is a complete tease. He flirts like a teenage boy, then walks away and leaves me panting.

"There are certain lines I don't cross, and fucking my employees is one of them."

His line from my interview plays on repeat in my head. After our San Francisco road trip, I looked up Vicka Neece. Like I had expected, she is beautiful, and very different from me. Blonde instead of brunette. Taller than me, and thin instead of curvy. She has that sophisticated scowl that I've never mastered. I can see why a man would go for her. And I can see, in the tattered remains of Marks Lingerie, what interoffice relationships can lead to.

I hadn't thought much about it while I was with Craig, but in the last five months as a single woman, Trey's stance on fraternization has haunted me. And right now, his belt is at eye level, the buckle begging to be freed, zipper yanked down, and all of Trey Marks's mysteries unveiled. My hand hovers above the belt. *It would be so easy.* I sigh and reach past it, for his waiting shirtsleeve, my hands quick and efficient as I fasten the cufflink. I look up at him and stick out my tongue.

"What is that for?" He extends the other hand, a smile playing across his lips.

"You. You and your ridiculous temptingness." The truth slips out before I can harness it in. I bite my bottom lip and look down at the cufflink, struggling more with getting this one through the hole.

"Oh good. I was worried I was losing my touch." He flips over his hands, offering them to me and I pull, getting to my feet.

"Nope. No worries there." I eye his suit. "So it's *this* kind of a dinner?"

"You were expecting the buffet? Keno and sweatpants?"

"Don't tempt me," I groan, moving past him and to the bathroom. "I've worn heels for, like, fourteen hours now."

"You don't have to come." He stands in the doorway and watches me. I grab a washcloth and rub it over my face, removing my makeup. I glance in the mirror, at my face, slightly pink from the hot water, and frown. Maybe I shouldn't be so surprised that Trey isn't trying to fuck me. Not when he sees me like this, in threadbare yoga pants and a shirt I borrowed from his suitcase without asking. That's what he gets for owning T-shirts that feel like suede and for booking us in adjoining rooms. I may be bringing his company success, but I'm not above blatantly stealing from his suitcase.

"I know Mira and her husband," he continues. "Why don't you take the night off? Get room service and a movie."

I turn off the water and glare at him in the mirror. "Her husband owns thirty-seven department stores in California. I don't care if you know Mira. Their first order, if we can get it, will be huge. No offense, but I'm not letting you screw it up."

"How can I *not* take offense to that?" He barks out a laugh, and follows me to my suitcase for a straightening iron.

"It's the truth." I plug in the iron. "And don't flirt with her."

"Oooh … jealous Kate. I knew you were in there somewhere."

"I'm not jealous, I'm sane. You don't know how you are, what you do to women. You say something casual to her, and her husband is going to bury you into next year—"

"Kate."

"…and he isn't going to care if—"

"KATE." He steps forward, pushing me against the bathroom counter, the line of his body hard, fitting perfect into my curves, one of his legs moving forward, in between mine, a stiff line of muscle against an area that hasn't gotten any attention since Craig in Hong Kong. "It'll be fine. I've met her husband before. Everything … will … be … *fine.*"

He drops his eyes from mine and down to my lips. His hands are resting on either side of me, flat upon the counter, caging me in, and I flinch when he moves just his thumbs, the scrape of them slowly caressing the sides of my hips. I can feel the delicate shift of air as he exhales, his eyes tracing over the lines of my lips, and I wet them in preparation. I should step aside, make a joke, mention the time. Instead, I close my eyes, my chin lifting, and wait for his kiss.

I hear his groan in the moment before he pushes off the counter, his body leaving mine, my skin suddenly cool without the heat of his touch. I open my eyes and he is there, against the wall of the bathroom, his hand worrying over his mouth, then crashing through his hair. He steps through the doorway, and then there is the slam of the connecting door, and I am alone.

I sag against the counter and let out a curse.

Him

My shoes clip across the hotel tile, a dominating sound that grounds me, another piece of the external appearance of control. I need the illusion, while inside, I fall to pieces.

My company needs her.
I need her.
And, unfortunately, so does my cock.

And that right there, is how things fall apart.

I step toward the maître d', and hope like hell she doesn't come to dinner.

Her

My hair up, I wear my best suit—a sexy YSL number that Trey bought for me in New York. He had groaned when I had stepped from the dressing room with it on. A very similar groan, in fact, to the one that had ripped from him in the bathroom.

Maybe he likes to torture himself. Or maybe he can only get himself off, and women are all just pawns in his ridiculous game of arousal.

Whatever the reason, this dinner is too important to let our misplaced sexual tension get in the way. I pass the hostess stand, my heels careful on the slick wood floors, and move through the tables, looking for him. In the back, in an elegant four-top overlooking The Strip, his eyes meet mine. He rises from his seat, and I step toward him.

Mira and Edward are from San Diego. She is a hugger, and I brace when she wraps her arms around my shoulders, her height putting her face uncomfortably close to my breasts. She's in a low-cut red dress, one that shows off impressive curves and olive skin. She's not traditionally pretty, but has the sort of face that is transformed when she smiles, her energy infectious. Her husband is more of the strong and silent type, a courteous gentleman who rises alongside Trey and extends a polite hand toward me. He is our mark—his upscale department stores the perfect home for our lingerie. We are in town for an expo, and Edward, apparently, loves any excuse to gamble.

"Trey was just telling us *all* about you." Mira leans forward, tucking a dark curl behind her ear and lowering her voice as if this is a secret of some sort. "He said you used to work at Lavern & Lilly."

"I did." I make a face. "It wasn't nearly as much fun as working for Marks."

She gives me a knowing smile. "Oh, I believe that. I worked with Trey before. I know how well he keeps his coworkers entertained." She steals a shrimp off the appetizer platter and turns to Trey. "Isn't that right, Trey?"

Trey attempts to give her a stern glare, one that loses its impact in the curve of his mouth. "It's not like that, Mira."

Goosebumps pop along my arm, and I study her face, the way she smirks at him before dipping the shrimp into sauce. From under the table, I feel Trey's hand settle on my thigh, his fingers squeezing, a brief warning that is entirely unneccesary.

"I'm sorry." I smile politely. "I didn't realize that you two worked together."

"It was at Bloomingdale's," Trey lifts his glass, the ice cubes settling in the amber liquid. "Mira worked in their accounts department."

"I seduced the poor boy," she interrupts grandly, holding up her wine glass to her husband, who lifts the bottle. I watch the dark red wine pour, and wonder exactly how many Bloomingdale's employees he went through. "And, honestly, he didn't have a chance."

"I wasn't exactly a boy, Mira." Trey lounges, his arm reaching behind my seat, the tips of his fingers brushing against my back. "I was twenty-four, same as you."

"I was wise beyond my years." She turns to her husband, who seems completely unconcerned about their history. "Wasn't I, babe?"

"Still are." He leans forward, setting down the wine bottle. "That's why you get along with me so well. I'm immature and you're ancient."

She scoffs, Trey chuckles, and I feel a combination of jealousy and confusion. I lift my drink and steal another glance at Mira, this one more apprising. I've seen a handful of Trey's dates, most the long-legged kind who don't concern themselves with breakouts, limp hair, or extra pounds. But Mira … she is a real woman, one whose nose is a little too big on her face, her features pleasant but not breathtaking, her body shape one that could shop at Lane Bryant as easily as Saks. She catches my eye and smiles, and her easy confidence is overwhelming. I swallow a sip of my mojito and search for something to say. "Edward, you met Mira through Bloomingdale's also?"

"I did." He had smile lines around his eyes, his head a thick pile of silver and gray. Somewhere in his fifties, with the same sort of lean build that Craig had. Probably a swimmer, or cyclist. "She was my account manager."

"How long were you with Bloomingdale's?" I ask Mira, taking a roll.

"God, two years. The longest two years of my life. But hey," she hugs Edward's arm, "it was worth it for this lug of sexuality." She glances at Trey. "Hell, relationship-building was the only real benefit of that place, right?"

He shifts in his seat and I pick up on his tension, the rigid tap of his finger against his spoon, the way he clears his throat. "Have you guys made it to Aspen yet this year?"

She leans forward, and launches into a long and moderately funny story about a ski trip. I cut my filet and watch Trey, wondering at his tension, the abrupt change in conversation. He glances at me and I meet his eyes, a question in the look. *What's going on?*

He looks away. Maybe it is just Mira's comment, the thinly veiled reference to Vicka and his relationship. But it seems like something else. He hadn't wanted me at this dinner at all. I glance at Mira and wonder if there is something else I am missing. Mira smiles at me, and I realize that the table has fallen quiet, everyone looking at me in the expectant way that follows a question. I swallow the bit of steak. "I'm sorry, what was the question?"

"Edward is leaving tonight, flying back home for a meeting. I was wondering if you could show me your new collections in the morning?"

"Of course." I smile, ignoring the hard press of Trey's ankle against mine. "I'd be happy to. Maybe we could grab lunch at Lago and go over it there."

"I could join you." Trey leans in, and I position the heel of my stiletto in the vicinity of his shoe, his foot quickly moving out of the way.

"That's not necessary." I beam at him. "You go do your manly stuff. Slot machines and whatnot. Let us have some girl time."

Mira giggles against her wine glass and Trey smiles tightly at me, a noticeable tic in his cheek. I take a long pull of merlot and wonder again, what the hell he is so worried about.

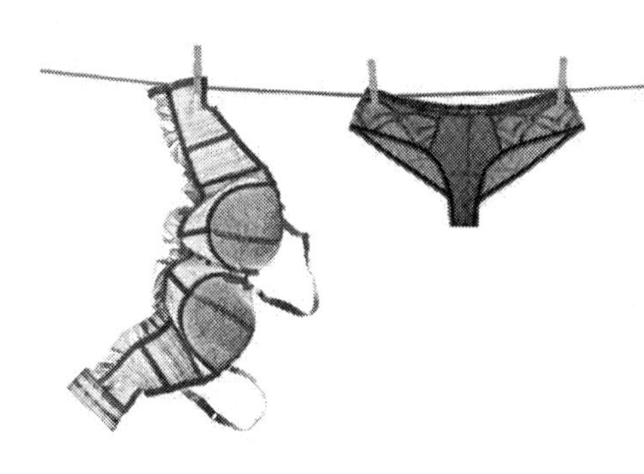

chapter 10
Him

Mira's hands grip Kate's shoulders and she kisses her cheek, smiling warmly and promising to see her tomorrow at noon. There is no way in hell that lunch is happening, but I'll take that up with Mira tonight, once I get her away from Kate. I aged five years during that dinner, my heart in my throat whenever Mira so much as opened her mouth. I'd forgotten how much, without a dick in her mouth, she talks. I'll fix that problem tonight.

She reaches for me, and I accept her hug, not reacting when she whispers her room number in my ear. I step away from her and extend a hand to Edward, his smile cordial. "Have a safe flight," I say.

"Certainly. I look forward to seeing you again soon." He releases my hand, and we step apart. I turn to Kate and reach for her hand, our goodbye involving another round of salutations before we are through the restaurant and into the casino.

"Want to play some slots?" I eye the blackjack tables, where Mira and Edward are headed.

"Sure," she replies cheerfully. "As long as you're paying."

"Of course." I place my hand on the small of her back, forcing myself to not caress the skin there, my steps brisk until we get to the private section of high limit slots. I pause, reaching into my wallet, and am stopped by Kate's stern look, her perky smile gone. I smell an ambush before she even opens her mouth.

"You prick with a dick." She crosses her arms over her chest and leans against the closest slot machine.

I look back down at my wallet, pulling out a handle of hundreds and buying myself a second to think. I close my wallet and stick it into my pocket. "What? I told you I knew her."

"*Knew* her? Yes, that's a bit of an understatement. Did you fuck *everyone* at Bloomingdale's?"

That earns her a smirk, my eyes taking a greedy trip down her body, lingering on the way her dress clings. "I managed some restraint at times."

"Don't," she warns, and God, I love it when she gets worked up.

I turn to the closest slot machine, feeding a bill into the machine in an attempt to keep myself from touching her. "It was a long time ago. She's married now. What difference does it make?"

"Her marriage didn't stop her from eye-fucking you across the table."

I glance at her, then push the button and watch the reels spin. "Easy, Kate. Your jealousy is showing."

She growls. "I'm not jealous, I'm intelligent. Our client is her husband. Are you too stupid to realize that he's not going to stock *anything* from someone his wife is attracted to?"

"I think you're wrong." I reach down and grab her hand, pulling her toward the machine, her struggle cute in a way that gets me hard as a rock. "Stop fighting me. I'm not fucking you against the reels. I just want you to push the button. Give me some lady luck." I slide my hand atop hers and gently push, the machine coming to life. She pauses her fight, watching the roll of lights, and slumps slightly when they come up mismatched. She goes to move away, and I move closer, trapping her, my chest against her back, her ass against me in a way that lights my senses on fire. "A few more." I speak against the back of her neck, her hair tickling my nose, my mouth close enough that, if I wanted to, I could drive her insane with just the brush of my lips against that skin. My hand still over hers, I give it a bit of pressure, using the excuse to push against her body, my cock pressing along the perfect curve of her ass, her inhale one that I will replay a hundred times over. "Watch it," I order.

"You're too close to me," she says, and her voice is husky, all fucking woman in every syllable of the words.

"You want me to move back?" I press the button under her hand, my hips thrusting again, and she sags back against me. God, she'd be so easy to please. In five minutes, I could make her mine. In ten minutes, she'd be calling me her god. In twenty, I could propose and she'd beg me for a lifetime more.

"Tell me, Kate. Tell me and I'll give you all of the space you want." Her hand moves beneath mine, slowly pushing the button, her ass arching against me, and I close my eyes in reverence, sending a thank you up to the God who created this perfect woman. She stiffens, and I open my eyes, almost falling forward as she spins toward me, all sexuality gone from her eyes, and I flinch when she shrieks, her arms flying into the air.

"We WON!" she yells, and if that is all it takes to get a woman out from under my touch, I need to up my fucking game.

I step back, glancing at the slot machine, which shows a trio of treasure chests. "Great," I mutter, watching her spin back to the machine, her chin tilting back, her finger raising as she finds the prize display.

"A thousand credits!" she shrieks again, her voice at a pitch that fighting cats frequent. "How much is a credit? Twenty-five—Trey, we won twenty-five thousand dollars!!!"

"Yippee," I say dryly, and I'd give all of it up to have her ass back where it belongs, flush against my cock. I glare at the machine, which blinks and dings with annoying cheer.

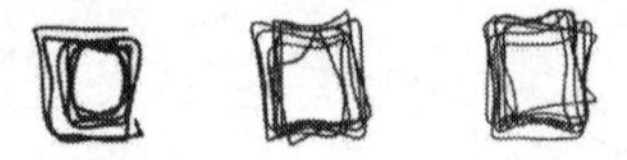

Room 1472. I stand at the double doors and contemplate my options. Mira isn't the type to lord sex over a sale, she'll have Edward order whatever we want, despite my cock's activities, or lack of it. I can certainly decline her offer, but that'd be a little ridiculous, given the rare times that our paths cross. I haven't been with her in two years, our last time in San Diego, three hours spent in every position known to man. She is my easy fix, the non-complicated sort that never pulls out a gun and steals my car. I eye her door and consider, one last time, returning to my room, to a jack off session and sleepless night, all one thin wall apart from Kate. I groan and reach forward, quickly rapping on the door, before I can change my mind.

A release will be good for me. It will get my mind off her. It will flush my system, and remind me of all of the reasons that Kate and I can't—won't—ever work.

The door swings open, and Edward stands there, his jacket and tie gone, his shirtsleeves rolled up, his feet bare on the plush carpet. "Trey." He steps back. "Come on in. Mira is waiting for us."

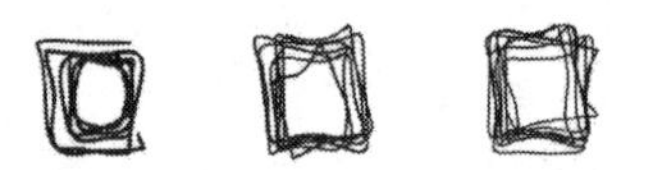

Two hours later, I close the door to the suite and walk down the hall, my jacket over my arm, my shirt rumpled from her nails, a button near the top cleanly ripped off. I examine the loose thread and grin, shaking my head at the thought of her. God, I forgot what a hellion she is, how she can pounce on your body and ride you like a fucking bull. I step on the elevator and press the button for my floor, catching my reflection in the metal doors. I look like a mess. I step closer to it, tilting my head to the side to examine the hickey that runs along my collarbone. I pull up my collar and frown, the mark not entirely hidden. Damn woman. I'll have to button up and wear a tie tomorrow. I am smiling as I step onto my floor, my mind in a better place than it had been two hours earlier. That's the value of Mira and Edward, even more than the orgasms. They are a reminder that there is nothing wrong with me, that we are all consenting adults who enjoy pleasure, in whatever form brings the most of it. If Mira likes getting two, or four, or ten cocks at once, that's her business and nobody else's. If I like a husband to watch me fuck his wife, or I enjoy competing for orgasms, why should society judge me for it?

I get it, though. I understand the stigma, the flinch of the mind when confronted with the idea. Hell, the first time Mira set it up, had I not been horny as hell, and twice as drunk, I'd have probably run the other way. But it had only turned me on more, thinking of fucking her in front of an audience, in front of another man, one who wanted her just as badly, or more, than I did. The competitiveness of it is an aphrodisiac, one so intense that normal sex can pale in comparison. Normal sex has, for a while, paled in comparison.

I stop in front of my room, and dig in my pocket for the key card, sliding it through the lock and pushing open the door, reaching for the light switch and stopping. On my bed, curled into a ball, her dark hair spread out on my pillow, is Kate. A remote hangs limply from her hand, her face illuminated by the screen, a black and white show running. I quietly pull the door closed and step into the bathroom, brushing my teeth and changing out of my clothes. I consider the shower and decide to wait, needing to get Kate back to her room before my cock comes back to life. I pull on workout pants and look for my T-shirt, getting frustrated as I dig through the suitcase. I am turning back to the closet when I see my shirt on her, the bright blue fabric loud against the white sheets. I smile despite myself, walking over and carefully taking the remote before turning off the television, the room falling dark. I pull back the covers, and slide my hands underneath her, gathering her into my arms, her body falling limply against my bare chest. I steal a moment and lean in, inhaling her scent, one of fresh soap and flowers, a combination I've gotten whiffs of but never fully sampled. I step slowly through the open door, into her dimly lit room, and make my way to her bed, the covers already pulled back and waiting for her. I stop, looking down at the bed, not yet ready to let her go, not yet ready to part. Maybe I should have left her on my bed. Maybe I should have laid down beside her and curled against her body. I could be there, my body pressed against hers, right now. I could spend all night with my mouth against her shoulder, and her legs against mine. I almost step back, but don't. It doesn't feel right, doing that tonight, not when I've spent hours with Mira and left her here alone.

I feel her stir and I glance down, watching her eyes open, the slow movement of them as they search the dark and find my face. She smiles, and my arms tighten around her. "I'm heavy," she whispers.

"Nah."

"How long have you been just standing here, staring at me?"

I can't stop the grin that stretches over my face. "It's creepy, right?"

"Totally creepy." She shifts, curling tighter against me, her hand fisting against my chest. Her eyes drop to the bare skin, then dart back to my face. "You're *naked*." She says the word with evil pride, as if she is a small child who has just caught an adult misbehaving and can't wait to tell someone.

I shake my head. "Sorry to disappoint you, but I'm wearing pants. I just couldn't find my *shirt*." I narrow my eyes at her, then pointedly drop the glare down to the shirt.

Her eyes roam over my shoulders, and she smiles. "I would apologize, but I'm enjoying the repercussions of my crime." She pats my chest. "How long are you planning on holding me up?"

I look down at the bed. "Not much longer." I bend over and extend her over the bed, smiling as she burrows into my neck, her deep inhale not much different than my own had been. I gently set her onto the mattress, and straighten, my arms sliding through hers, when her grip clamps down on my forearm, her eyes going from sleepy to sharp.

"Trey?" My stomach clenches at the accusatory way she says my name. "Why do you smell like Mira's perfume?"

I meet her eyes, and in that connection, she knows. She doesn't know everything, but she knows I fucked her, and that is enough.

  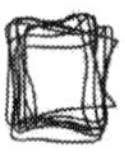

Kate pushes out of my arms, sliding across the bed, to the other side. "Kate," I plea. This is bad. This is fucking *bad*, made worse because I can't explain it to her.

"Shut up," she snaps, her hands pulling at the sheet, covering herself as if she is naked. "I—" She looks away. "I literally have *nothing* to say to you."

"It didn't mean anything." I press the fingers of my hand into my forehead, rubbing at the stress points there. Why didn't I take a fucking shower? But the answer to that is easy: Kate Martin was in my bed.

"That makes it even worse!" Her eyes widen, and in them, I see her hurt. "What if Edward finds out?"

Edward reaches down, gripping her chin and lifting it, her eyes meeting his, the rock of her body not stopping their eye contact. "Tell me," he orders. "Do you like how he fucks you?"

"Yes sir," she gasps, and he smiles, pulling down the zipper of his pants.

"Edward isn't going to find out." *Edward knows*, I want to scream. *Stop worrying about work, or our precious order. Everything there is fine.* I have a brief moment of insanity, one where I want to tell her everything, to try and explain it all. But I don't, I can't. This isn't my secret to tell. There are other lives involved, other reputations at stake. Would Mira care? Probably not. But that's not my call to make. And even if it were, could I tell Kate? Could I really tell her that Edward and I took turns with Mira? That he held back her hair and told her to suck my cock?

I can't. There is no way. Tears leak out of the corners of her eyes and I feel a piece of me break. "God dammit, Kate," I say softly. "Just forget it. Please."

She rolls over on the bed, her back to me. "Go away, Trey. Just let me sleep."

Leaving her is the last thing I want to do. We need to discuss this, to talk this through, to get back to *us*. But it's hard to talk through it when I can't explain my actions, my motivations. I have nothing to say, no defense to give. I move back a step, then another. I wait for a long moment in the doorway, considering what this will do to our relationship, what this will mean. She doesn't turn, and I pull the adjoining door closed, the act feeling almost ceremonial in its division of us.

Maybe this is it, the death of our possibilities. Maybe I need this reminder of the differences between her and me, of all of the ways that—even without the company dividing us—we would never work. Maybe I should use this excuse, this opportunity, to mentally push away.

She won't ever accept what happened between Mira, Edward, and me. I swallow that reality and head to the shower, anxious to wash away everything.

If this evening was lingerie, it'd be expensive, the kind that seems worth the price tag but isn't, the kind that leaves your wallet empty and your mind fucked.

Her

It's official. The man's penis only knows stupid mistakes. First that crazy mugger woman, and now this—a married woman. I bet Edward wasn't even out of the hotel before Trey was knocking on her door. Had I even been a thought? You'd think if the man was going to destroy everything, he might have at least *glanced* my way, at least *considered* me before risking the wrath of our client by sleeping with his wife.

I lay in the dark room, gripping a pillow against my chest, and listen to the click of the air conditioner as it comes on. My heart gallops against my chest, my arms tighten around the pillow, and I want to scream, but instead, I only growl. I tell myself that it's not jealousy, but it is. It's jealousy, and regret, and months of sexual frustration. Why her? Why not a Vegas hooker, or a horny tourist? Why risk this account, one that we need, all to fuck an ex-girlfriend? If he's so cavalier about the risk to the company, then why not date me?

I roll onto my back and force my arms to relax, to flop back on the mattress. My mind relaxes slightly. Maybe it's because, despite all of his flirting, and our latent chemistry—I'm not his type. Maybe all of my sexual tension is one-sided, and he's operating in a purely platonic world where he flirts for the sheer fun of it, and is oblivious to the delusional fantasies of my starved sex drive. I consider knocking on his door and just asking him, flat out, to explain himself, but abandon the thought. My nerves are too frayed to have that conversation face-to-face, in an environment where all of my reactions and emotions will be seen. No way to play the cool, aloof girl in that scenario. I roll over, pick up my phone, and compose a text.

Are you attracted to me?

Women aren't supposed to ask questions like that. We should be pursued; we should always know our power. But I don't. And I need to know. He's my best friend, and we shouldn't have to tiptoe around our feelings. We should be able to have a rational and open discussion about this ridiculously huge thing that has been dominating my spare thought processes for the last … hell … even before Craig and I ended.

My phone beeps, and I pick it up off the bedspread.

— *Devastatingly so.*

I stare at the response, my heart pulled between elation and fear, a flood of new questions arising. I mull them over and wait for him to ask me the same question, but the phone stays dark. Should I tell him that I feel the same way? No. I can't. I roll onto my back and hesitantly type out the next question, reading over it several times before I press send.

Then why aren't we together?

I lay the phone on my chest and stare at the ceiling. Part of me regrets bringing this up. What if he wants to start a relationship? Do I even want that? I've known him for fourteen months, and he hasn't had a steady girlfriend that entire time. Would he be good boyfriend material? Can he be loyal? Is he romantic? Too many questions and no answers. I pick up my phone and double-check that my text was delivered. It shouldn't take this long to respond, to provide a simple answer to such an important question. I close my eyes and attempt to relax, focusing on my feet and slowly moving up my body, relaxing one muscle group at a time, my arms loose and rubbery by the time my phone finally dings. I slowly roll to my side and lift my phone, reading his response.

— *too much at risk*

The brevity of it irritates me, as if he didn't have the energy to go into greater detail. But in those four words, I understand his stance. It's the same logic I've told myself a hundred times. He went down this road with Vicka, and his company had tanked as a result. Dating Trey could ruin Marks Lingerie's forward progress, not to mention our friendship. In some ways our bond seems unflappable. In other ways, we seem as fragile as glass. No one else can hurt me like this. No one else's opinion is as important. No one else can break my heart as easily as he could mend it.

If he thinks there is too much at risk, then fine. I can cross Trey Marks off my list of prospects and dive back into the world of dating. I can find someone else, someone better for me, someone without consequences. I can find a relationship that, if it ends, won't destroy every other part of our lives.

I don't need Trey in my bed, as my boyfriend. I can be happy having him everywhere else.

I don't know if it's a lie or not, and in this moment, I don't care. I wrap my hand around my phone, slide it under the pillow, and close my eyes.

I wake to a note from Mira, one slipped under my door, her handwriting big and flowery. In it, she cancels our lunch, full of apologies and promises to find me on a future trip. The note is attached to a purchase order, one that Trey must have prepared, the unit count enough to make our quarter, if not our year. I roll my eyes and toss it onto the bed.

There is a knock on the adjoining door and I open it, giving Trey a tight smile and returning to my suitcase, the zipper difficult. He pushes down on the lid and I work it closed. "Thanks."

"Certainly." He is in khakis and a polo, the bright blue cotton setting off his tan. This is country-club Trey, the preppy look that used to get me hot, the clean-cut exterior so easily twisted with just one smoldering eye-fuck. *Used* to get me hot. Today I am a new woman, one perfectly content in my Best Friend and Creative Director roles, one who doesn't wonder what he looks like naked, or what that delicious mouth is capable of.

He strolls over to the bed, reaching forward and picking up the items from Mira. "What's this?" He flips over the top page, his head dropping as he reads over it. "I thought she was sending this to me."

"Did you see the note?" I say brightly. "She cancelled our lunch."

"Yeah. I told her to." He glances at me. "I figured you wouldn't want to eat with her after…" He grimaces. "You know."

"Oh yes." I smile again, and his eyes narrow. "I know." I step forward and pluck the pages back. "I would have been fine having lunch with her. I don't need you running around and rearranging my schedule."

"I'm sorry." He doesn't sound sorry. He sounds unsettled, which makes me ridiculously happy. I can do this. I can be the cool girl, the friend who doesn't care that her friend, her boss, is *devastatingly* attracted to her. I can roll my eyes at his slutty antics and go off and marry a different Prince Charming. We can build this company, be friends, and I can have smoking hot sex and babies who have nothing to do with Trey Marks.

I can have it all. I can. I will.

He looks at me and I look at him, and if he kisses me right now, I would fall apart under his touch.

He holds the gaze, and I look away, afraid of what my eyes might show.

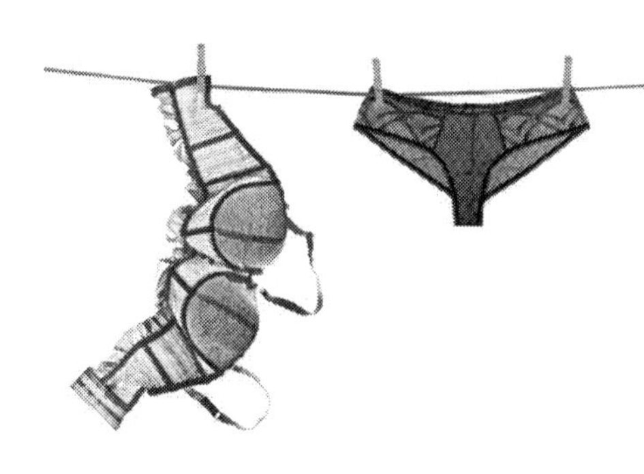

chapter 11
Her

Four months later, I find my prince in a coffee shop downtown. Or rather, he finds me.

"Kate?" I look up and swallow the sip of coffee, my eyes darting over all of the details.
Soft brown hair, void of product.
Pale green eyes, the kind that smile. He wears glasses, and I unconsciously touch my own, glad that I'd skipped the contacts today.
His features are as advertised, a classic profile set off by straight, perfect teeth and an adorably crooked nose.
A blue sweater, the fabric snug around a manly build, his height tall enough that I can wear heels and still be shorter.

I rise, and extend a hand. "Hi. You must be Stephen." We shake hands, and it is a good handshake, firm but not businesslike, his hands soft and warm, everything about him reassuringly conservative. "Please, sit down."

He pulls out the opposite seat and settles into it, and there is a moment of awkward silence, one where I sip my coffee and he straightens his glasses, and I can't, for the life of me, think of a single thing to say. Our eyes meet, he smiles, and I laugh despite myself.

"This is my fifth blind date," he admits. "You'd think I would have learned something aside from my name by now."

"My eighth." I smile. "You look like you recently bathed, so you don't really have to say anything. You're already ahead of the rest." It's a lie, and he knows it, but he leans forward and conversation begins to flow.

"So you work in retail?" He tucks his hands into his pockets as we walk, his head down, ear cocked to me.

"Sort of. I work for an undergarments company. We supply to retail shops and some high-end chains."

"Undergarments. Like underwear, hosiery?"

I nod, pulling back my hair into a low ponytail. "Yes. Less hosiery and more of the delicate items. Bras, panties, garters, babydolls. The sexier stuff. Our lines are fairly provocative."

Trey would have made a sly comment, worked a compliment in, but Stephen only nods, his face a mask of concentration. "And what do you do for the company?"

"I model."

The joke falls flat, and he only nods, as if I am *serious*, as if there is any chance of my frame on a cover. "I'm joking," I hurry. "I'm the Creative Director; I'm responsible for the overall vision and the execution of it." I feel the burst of pride that comes whenever I say my title.

"That's nice." We take the path into the park, a canopy of trees providing a break from the sun. His arm brushes mine, a reminder of where I am and who I am with. Not Trey, who is accustomed to my long stretches of silence, but this man, who probably thinks I'm odd. I am trying to think of something to say when he speaks. "How long have you been there?"

I relax a bit. "A year and a half."

"Do you enjoy it?"

"I do," I say honestly. "Trey is very good to work for. We get along well."

"That's nice."

I ask him what he does, and learn that he is an oral surgeon. A fancy dentist, as he says. He travels two days a week, has a rescued dog, and a mother in Chula Vista. We both love sushi and hate Star Wars. We are both Words With Friends enthusiasts, and—unless I am misreading the look in his eye—we both want to see each other again.

We end our walk at the parking lot. Ahead of us, my bright red Mercedes convertible sits, a gift from Trey when we hit last year's sales goal. He reaches into his pocket and a new Volvo SUV beeps. "That's me."

He turns to me and smiles. It's a nice smile, one warm and friendly. He steps forward and my heart speeds up. A kiss. My first kiss since Craig. Would I remember how to do it properly?

He extends a hand. "Thank you for meeting me. And for not being a serial killer."

I laugh, and take his hand. "Agreed. I was actually planning on being a serial killer but decided against it. My day is kind of full. Meetings." I smile and I think he can tell I'm joking.

He steps back and waves. "I'll call you. If that is okay."

"It is." I return the wave, and wait for him to turn, to walk away before I dig into my pockets for my keys.

"You told him you were a serial killer?" The wind ruffles the papers in Trey's hand, and I glance toward them worriedly.

"Can we step inside?" I ask. "You're going to lose something."

He pushes the door open with his foot, holding it in place as he waves me through. "Is that what you wore?"

"No, I went home and changed," I say tartly. "Yes, this is what I wore. It's nice." The questionable outfit—a Jones New York skirt suit, one I had paired with a sweetheart top. Not the most casual of first date attire, but I'd met Stephen in the middle of a work day. A mini-dress hadn't exactly seemed appropriate.

"Yes," he agrees, pulling the door closed, the wind quieting, the sound of sports coming from another room. "It's nice. Let's go into the kitchen."

I pull off my suit's jacket and hang it over his stairway banister, pulling the hair away from my neck and following him to the kitchen, where he straddles a stool and flips over the first page of the contract. "You don't want to dress *nice* when you go on a date, Kate."

"Sorry," I respond tartly. "We can't all work from home during the playoffs." I open his fridge, reaching down to the bottom drawer, where he keeps my Diet Coke. I grab one and push the drawer closed with my foot, elbowing the door shut before turning to him. His eyes flick up to my face. "Grab me one?"

"A Diet Coke?" I raise my eyebrows. He doesn't drink diet. More than that, he scoffs at any man who does.

"There are regular ones in the same drawer. Underneath yours."

I yank open the door and bend back over, digging through the ice cold pile of bottles, getting frustrated when I can't … I look over my shoulder and see Trey settled back on the stool, one foot up on the adjoining stool, his eyes fixed on my ass. I straighten and his eyes jump to mine. "What?" he asks.

"You don't have any regulars in there."

"Maybe they're in the other drawer, to the left of it. But arch your back this time. And moan a little."

I sling my can of Diet Coke at his head, and he catches it, one-handed, a mischievous smile lighting up his face. "What? I'm thirsty!"

"I'm sure you are," I grumble, kicking the door shut and leaning against the counter. "I ought to sue your ass for sexual harassment. "

"Wear that suit in court and no one will believe you."

"It's not that bad." I glare at him and steal my soda back, tapping the lid before I crack it open.

"What's underneath it?"

I ignore him and push the contract forward. "Sign this so I can get out of your hair."

"Fine. Come over here and explain it to me." He drops his foot from the other stool and pulls it out, his hand fishing in the top drawer of the island for a pen.

Trey Marks has several sides, but his business mode is the most tempting. It's the seriousness that takes over his face, the somber tone, that smooth tongue that delivers words like *boning*, *peephole*, and *thong* without hesitation. I've taken advantage of it, stocking our meetings with female buyers, their reactions similar to my own, the entire room one big estrogen explosion by the time he slips his hands into his pockets and strolls out.

Now, I move to his side of the island and perch on the stool, leaning forward and pulling the cover page back into place. I have barely begun my explanation when I feel the tip of his pen pulling up the edge of my skirt. I stall, my eyes dropping to my thighs, the skirt inching higher, past my knees, now my thighs. My hose ends, my skin pale against the edge of the black lace, and my breath catches when the tip of the metal crosses onto my skin. "Easy…" he says slowly. "I'm just checking…" He slides the pen along the top of my stocking, until he reaches the garter clip. "What are these, the Mirabellas?"

"Yes." I reach down to tug the skirt back into place and he swats away my hands.

"Put your hands on the counter, Kate. This isn't going anywhere."

This isn't going anywhere? This has already gone somewhere it shouldn't.

"I'm not touching you, Kate. Calm down." He sounds so mild, as if he is examining packaging samples or marketing copy.

I let out a frustrated breath. "What are you doing?" We don't do this. This is not playful flirtation, not when I am wet from just the touch of his pen.

"Put your hands on the counter. Flat. Palms down. Trust me."

In eighteen months, he has ordered me to do many things. I almost always obey. Not always because I want to, but because I like to. When he uses that voice, it does something inside of me. Something that felt—back when I was engaged to Craig—wicked. *Put your hands on the counter. Flat. Palms down.* I glance down at his pen, the metal tip of it next to the lace of my stocking. He drags the point lightly against my skin and I close my eyes. I carefully place my hands on the cool surface of his counter, my fingers spreading over the marble, lines of silver and blue across the giant expanse of white. *Trust me.* In some ways, I trust him with my life. In other ways, *these* ways, I wouldn't put anything past him. Will he lower his mouth to mine? *Maybe.* Will he slide his hands up my sweater and brush his fingers over my breasts? *I hope so.*

"You know we've had some complaints of the elastic getting

stretched out on these." He slides the pen underneath the top of the stocking, his eyes on the motion, and I watch as he tilts his head, watching the nylon stretch. "Have you experienced that?"

"No."

"I'm going to slide my hand under here."

"Why?"

"I want to." His eyes lock with mine, his hand not hesitating as he sets the pen down on the counter, and reaches his hand forward. I can hear the roll of the pen as it moves toward the edge, but I can't look away, can't breathe, as he holds my eyes with his. "Is that okay, Kate?"

His hand closes on my thigh, a warm grip of ownership, and I close my eyes.

"Is that okay, Kate?"

I can't answer him. If I speak, I'll beg. If I say anything at all, he will know just how badly I want him.

He slides his hand along the inside of my leg, his palm along the lace, his thumb on my bare skin, playing with it as he moves. "Open your legs, Kate. Uncross them."

"Trey." It is the best defense I can manage. I think of Mira, of smelling her perfume, and I reach out to grab his wrist, to pull it away—

"Just your right hand on the counter." He moves off his stool, coming closer, and I can smell his cologne, feel the brush of his shirt against my sleeve. I remove one hand from the counter, my body swiveling to him, and my knees brush against the thigh of his jeans. "This is market research, Kate. I'm just examining the product. Now, open your legs before I pull them apart myself."

I open them. I let my feet hang loose from the stool and open my knees, one heel dropping to the floor, the sound loud, my shoulders jumping in response. I lift my eyes to him, and he slowly nods, holding me with his stare. He doesn't smile, he doesn't blink, and I'd be surprised if he is even breathing. For a moment, both of us just *are*. Then he drops his head, and I watch as his second hand joins in, both tracing over the place where my garters clip to my stockings. He runs his fingers up, my shirt stopping his hand, the fabric restricted by my butt on the stool. He softly clicks his tongue against his teeth. "Stand up."

"I'm not standing up."

"Kate."

"Stop saying my name. I'm not standing up." If I stand up, then my panties are going to end up coming off, and this is going to go to a very bad place, a place that I have been wanting for over a year, but that doesn't matter right now, none of that matters right now, because this isn't just Trey, this is the owner of Marks Lingerie, and if he—he slides his hands underneath my skirt, and I gasp when his fingers reach the bottom edge of my underwear. My other heel hits the floor.

He tilts his head, his fingers caressing the silk, then the top of my thighs, then the detailed edge between them. "Are these from the fall collection?"

"Winter." The word whispers out of me. "Please stop." I'm so wet. He hasn't even done anything, hasn't even kissed me, and I am so needy, so desperate.

"You want me to stop?" His fingers stop their play above my thighs, and he slides one slow, sure hand in between my legs, his touch soft and teasing, my legs opening wider despite myself, my hips thrusting upward, begging for him to—

He brushes his fingers across my clit, and I whimper. He slides his fingers lower, in between my legs, pressing into the damp area, and when he says my name, it is a swear across his lips. "Stop," I beg.

"I don't know if I can."

Him

I mean it when I say it. I don't know if I can stop. Not when she sits on the edge of the stool, her skirt pushed up, knees spread, her legs limp and hanging open. I stand before her, one hand squeezing and caressing her thigh. My other hand is seriously fucking with my mind. It plays with her pussy, her sweet pussy, a thin bit of my lingerie the only thing between my skin and hers. I'm terrified to move those panties aside; I'm terrified, if I touch her bare heat, if I feel the smooth skin or silky hair, that I will lose all control. If I push one finger, or two, inside of her … god damn. How will I stop myself from yanking at my belt, my zipper? How will I stop myself from freeing my cock and thrusting it inside of her? I am just seconds away from being able to have her, from gripping her ass and pulling her onto me, from pushing deep inside and fully owning this incredible woman. I could fist her hair and kiss her mouth. I could taste her, have her, please her. I could spread her open on my counter and tease every part of her with my tongue, my fingers, my dick. I could tell her how I feel and plead for her heart. I could come inside of her, and have her for the rest of my fucking life.

I could scare her away and lose her forever.

Stop, she'd said. I pull my hand away and straighten, putting one foot, then two, between us. I have to stop. I have to. Against the zipper of my jeans, my cock hates me even more.

I turn away from her and take a breath, schooling my features, willing the raw need to leave my eyes. Had she seen it? How badly I want her? Of course she had. Touching her? What the fuck was I thinking?

It had been the news of her date that had broken my restraint, the way she had bounded inside, full of stories and smiles, as if this guy was a possibility, as if he could, in any way, make her happy. I had seen hope in her eyes, and a panic switch in my heart had tripped.

Stop, she'd said. I turn back to her and attempt the playful tone that has gotten me out of a hundred situations. "And you say I don't follow directions."

She faces the island, the contracts spread out before her, and I know what I will see when I step beside her—control. My beautiful girl loves it, the hiding of emotion, so many interactions a game where her words don't match her features, and her meanings are never easily deciphered.

"Why did you care what I was wearing under my suit?" Her head doesn't turn to me, it stays tilted down, over the contract, her fingers busy, pulling off and reaffixing SIGN HERE stickers that aren't needed.

"I wanted to know if you were at least giving the guy some sort of effort."

That causes her head to turn, and she looks at me as if I am mental. "It was our first date. A *coffee* date. He wasn't going to see anything under my suit."

"Because … you told him you were a serial killer?" I feign confusion, furrowing my brow and earning a smile from her.

"Because it was a FIRST DATE," she intones. "We didn't even kiss." She taps the top of a page. "Come sign."

"He didn't kiss you?" This is alarming, and I sit, pulling the first page toward me and scrawling my signature across the bottom.

"No. Which kind of surprised me." She tilts her head, watching me sign the second page, a slow smile spreading over her lips. "It was kind of nice, actually. He was such a gentleman about it."

This I don't need. Her gushing, her starry eyes, her fucking "gentleman." What was the point of having IT hack into her eHarmony profile if it ended up matching her with comparable men? They were supposed to make her profile such a train wreck that she was only paired with losers. "What does he do? This gentleman of yours?"

"He's a dentist," she tosses out, pushing another page in my direction. "Or a tooth surgeon. Whatever that's called."

"An oral surgeon?" I ask, my hand tightening on my pen.

"Yes!" She snaps. "That's it. Thanks." Any effect that my hands had had on her has apparently disappeared. She now seems a hundred percent focused on this stupid contract and this dumb date of hers.

"Did you like him?" I ask the question as casually as I can, my pen biting into the soft paper, my scrawl rougher than usual.

"I think so. He's a lot better than the other guys. And I'm pretty tired of looking."

"That sounds like the recipe for success. A guy who's better than a pile of idiots, and a woman tired of looking." I shove the final page toward her and stand. "Does love have any piece of that equation?"

"It was our *first* date, Trey," she calls out. "Give it a few more dates."

The next question I shouldn't ask; it's not any of my business, not appropriate among coworkers, and not even among friends. I stalk my way to the fridge, fighting it. Still, right before I find and crack a beer open, it comes. "When are you planning on fucking him?"

She is standing, gathering the papers, a paperclip in hand, when the question hits. She doesn't look at me. "That's none of your business."

"I just don't want you to rush into it. It's only been … what? Nine months since you and Craig—"

"Shut up." She turns toward me, her hands reaching back to the counter and she hoists herself onto the marble as if she was fifteen. "If I wanted you to, you'd fuck me right now." She pulls up her skirt, working it over her thighs, and spreads her knees far enough apart that I can see the pale pink of her panties, a match to the garter straps. A year ago, we'd argued over the name of its color. A year ago, I'd stared at a sample set and envisioned them on her. "So don't lecture me about my virtue or if I'm ready. I think you just don't want me to fuck anyone else."

I try to keep my eyes on her face, but it is difficult when her legs are open, her words challenging me, and I am almost in reach of her. "Don't tempt me, Kate."

"Am I right, Trey?" She drags my name along her tongue and it has never sounded so sexy in its life.

"You're my best friend. I'm trying to watch out for you."

"So you *don't* want to fuck me." She lifts her chin, pulling self-consciously at her blouse, and her knees start to close.

"Stop." I step forward, my hands settling on her knees and pushing them apart, her body opening like a flower for me, that fucking pink silk flashing at me from between her thighs. I pull my gaze from it and back to her face. "If you want me to *fuck* you, Kate, just say the word. Don't ever be confused over whether I want that. There's not anything on Earth I want as badly as you. I'd love to know if the chemistry that we have … if it could be how I imagine it."

One of her hands moves, a tentative reach that runs along my right collarbone before settling on my chest. "And if it isn't?" Her eyes dart to mine, and the fact that there's insecurity in them breaks my heart.

"God, I hope it isn't. I hope it's terrible. It would make our lives so much easier." I smile, and her eyes warm, and holy shit—this may actually happen. I wet my lips and say the one thing that may destroy it all.

"But I meant what I texted you, back in Vegas. It's too risky." I slide my hands off of her knees, my fingers memorizing the contours of her legs, the silky feel of the stockings. I step back and put my hands in my pockets before I make another mistake with them. "There's too much—"

"At stake," she finishes, her knees meeting, and she pushes off of the counter and down to the floor, gripping the edge for support. "Yeah, that sounds familiar." She bends down and pulls on one heel, and then the other. "When do you leave for New York?"

"Tomorrow night." I hesitate, second-guessing my next move. "Want to come?"

She shakes her head, reaching for her purse. This must be it, the end of her visit. I used to like the solace, the moment when I would step inside my home and hear NOTHING. Now, it only feels lonely.

She pauses next to me, on her way to the door. "We good?"

"Always." I lean into her and she brushes her lips against my cheek. "Drive safe."

"I will." She squeezes my arm, and then, her heels clipping out of the kitchen, she is gone.

"We good?" If my answer had been lingerie, it'd have been a bustier. Deceptive as hell.

chapter 12
Her

I turn on the shower and unclip the garter belt, rolling the expensive hosiery down my legs and stepping out of my damp panties, leaving the pile of lingerie on the floor of my bathroom, the rest of my undressing done with less ceremony. I consider the suit, then toss both the jacket and the skirt in the direction of my bed. He's right, it is ugly. And I'll never be able to wear that skirt again without thinking of his pen pushing up the fabric, his hands so close behind it. Naked, I open up the door and step into the shower, closing my eyes as the hot water hits my skin.

I don't know what to do with him. I'd almost begged him. I'd almost said I didn't care about commitments and risks and had him take me to his bedroom right there.

Put your hands on the counter. Flat. Palms down. God, the places my mind had run. I could feel the heat of him when he had moved behind me, the brush of him against me. If he had knelt, had lifted my skirt and bared my ass, run his fingers along the Brazilian cut of my underwear, if he had dragged my panties to the side … I slide my hand down, to my swollen clit, and softly brush my fingers over it. Had he realized how wet I was? How badly I wanted him? Even now, I throb at the thought of it, the huskiness in his voice, the dominant way his hand had closed around my thigh.

"I'm going to slide my hand under here." I rub a slow circle around my clit and reach for the handheld shower attachment. I flip the control and

water pulsates from the head, a small groan falling from my lips as I press it between my legs, the hot water strumming across my clit, my legs tightening in response. I brace a hand against the tile wall, my eyes closing as I remember the look in his eyes when his hands had slid under my skirt, when his fingers had explored the edges of my panties, when his hand had cupped me, his gentle fingers pushing the damp fabric inside of me. All he had had to do was move the piece of fabric aside. One tiny movement. One curve of his digits, and I would have gripped his shoulders and sobbed out his name, promised him anything, and begged him for everything. Replace those fingers with his cock, and I would have sold him my soul.

"Open your legs, Kate. Uncross them." I need him in an unnatural way. I need him to push apart my thighs and put his mouth on me. I need him to suck on my clit and tease me with his fingers; I need him to gather me against his chest and push his cock inside of me. I want to look down and see his bare cock, to watch it against my skin, the thrust of it, the tight clench of his abs, his hands on my hips, the burn in his eyes when he buries it fully. Just the thought of it makes my legs tremble, my hips thrust, and I grind against the shower head like a dog in heat. I bite my lip. Sometimes, with just a certain look, I can sense his arousal. That look always makes me think of his cock, thickening inside of his pants, growing stiff, the hard ridge of him pushing against the fabric. I tilt my hips forward, giving a sigh of pleasure as my legs nearly buckle, my orgasm close. I imagine him standing up from his desk, that look deepening, his hand pulling on his zipper, pulling out his cock.

"Open your legs before I pull them apart myself." He had said that to me. My Trey. He had given that order, and I had spread my legs for him. Had he seen my panties? Had he seen the way that they stuck to me, the way that I had trembled? I imagine him stepping forward, his head tilting, eyes searching, his fingers pulling my panties to the side, and all of me, swollen and pink and wet. He would look up, and that look, that look in his eyes—I come from the idea, the orgasm violent, my fingers sliding against the tile, my body tensing, back rounding, and it is long and hard when it blooms, a wave of pleasure that shudders through me, my cries drowned out by the water, my pleasure extended by the spray. When I finally sink back against the

wall, I am numb, my emotions spent, my body limp, my head a fog of orgasmic bliss.

It's just fantasies. Fantasies that will have no life. Fantasies that only belong in private moments between myself and my fingers, my toys, my showerhead. Eventually, I'll have someone new, someone who will steal my heart and take over my mind and erase all of these ridiculous thoughts.

I reach and turn the handheld off, closing my eyes and stepping under the overhead's hot spray.

A month later, the woman sits quietly before me, her heels crossed at the ankles, her hands in her lap. She is a few years younger than me, and I can see it in her innocence, her nervous eyes, the tap of her dark nails against her black jeans, the fidget with her smartwatch. I look down at her resume, one fairly impressive, and that aligns well with the graphic designer job. I ask about her current employer, and she begins to speak, pausing when there is a gentle knock on my office door.

"Good morning," Trey's voice fills my office, and I glance sharply at him.

"Good morning," I say mildly, in an attempt to mask my irritation. "I'll be through in a few minutes."

He steps inside, and I stifle a groan. "Ms. Cone, this is Trey Marks, our owner. Trey, this is Chelsea Cone."

"We've met before." He extends a hand and she rises to her feet, her cheeks flaring bright pink. I watch in interest. "It's nice to see you again. Thank you for coming in."

"My pleasure." She keeps standing and I look at Trey.

"I'm almost done here, Trey."

"Of course." He smiles at me, and there is something there, a message of some kind, but I miss it. "Could you see me when you wrap up? There's an issue with the Brazil order, I just need you to look at it."

The 'Brazil order' is our code. Something is wrong, and I cycle through the morning's events, the outstanding issues, all of the things that might have gone wrong. I nod. "I'll be there shortly."

When he leaves, the color in her cheeks fades to normal, her return to her seat almost more of a collapse, and I eye her carefully. "Is everything okay?"

"Yes. I'm sorry. I'm just feeling lightheaded."

I close the binder holding her resume. She's the strongest candidate so far, and I choose my words carefully, my mind distracted by Trey and his Brazil order. "Thank you for coming in. We'll make a decision on this position by the end of the week."

She rises, and I walk her to reception, then head straight to Trey's office.

"What's wrong?" I pull the door closed, thinking of our factory shipment, the pending patent on our new hook closures, the civil lawsuit against our silk manufacturer.

"Don't hire her." He sits in his leather office chair, one elbow on the arm, his hand playing with the stubble on his jaw.

It is so unexpected that it takes me a moment to catch up. "Who? Chelsea?"

"Yes."

"Why?"

His hand falls from his mouth and grips his desk, pulling his chair forward. "I have a history with her."

Between Vicka and Mira, I've seen the women Trey has histories with. They are strong, confident women, nothing like sweet, meek Chelsea. "What kind of history?" I ask carefully. "You dated?"

"No. Just a one-time thing." He nods toward one of his chairs. "Sit down. You're freaking me out, looming over me like this."

"You had a one-night stand with her?" I laugh uncertainly. "Really? Are you sure?"

"It wasn't exactly a one-night stand, and yes, I'm quite sure of who I have *fucked*, Kate." The emphasis he gives the word sends a dark tingle down my spine.

"So … you don't want me to hire her?" I have so many questions, all inappropriate for this moment.

"I think I've made my opinion on interoffice fraternization clear."

I meet his eyes, and something thicker than tension passes between us. Yes, his position on that is clear. Crystal clear.

I nod slowly. "Okay. I'll find someone else."

"Thank you, Kate."

Just the way he says my name hurts.

Her

The restaurant is one of those places that takes farm-to-table a little too seriously, the waiter launching into an extended monologue as soon as we sit down. He delivers us each mini-plates with something from the chef designed to "awaken our palates," something we should think of as a "delightful journey for the tongue." I automatically glance at Trey, ready for his dirty take on the phrase, but he isn't looking at me. The smirk is there, but it's directed at his date—Chelsea—who blushes, her hand nervously playing with the end of her braid. I move to Stephen, who dubiously lifts the cracker and dips it into the gooey caramel-colored sauce. I look down at my own sampling, and the knot in my stomach fully forms.

The wine is delivered, along with a second monologue about the appetizer options, one Trey fully ignores, his mouth at the blonde's ear, his arm draped over her chair, the edge of those fingers playing with her bare shoulder. When he finally looks up, the speech is over, and the wine is poured. I reach for my glass and Trey stands, stilling my action.

"A toast," he says, lifting his glass. "It's been three months for the two of you, correct?" He glances from Stephen to me and smiles warmly.

"That's correct." Stephen extends his glass and half-rises in his seat.

"To three months, and many more." Trey lifts his glass, and we toast, my eyes meeting his as our glasses touch. I narrow my eyes slightly but he only smiles. "Congrats, Kate."

"It's three months," I say as sweetly as I can manage. "Not exactly toast-worthy." We all return to our seats and I watch Chelsea cup both sides of her wine glass as if it's a warm mug of coffee. I don't need to ask how long they have been dating. I can tell you that with psychotic clarity. Two and a half months. Two weeks after Stephen and I became official, she showed up at the office, a Kate Spade slung over her shoulder, yoga pants and a midriff-baring tank top on. She had waved a cheery hello at me and bounced into Trey's office, his door quickly shut, blinds drawn. Apparently Trey hadn't wanted to hire her, yet had wanted to rekindle their past. I had stared at an inventory report and tried to think of anything other than what was happening in there. It had been the longest twenty-two minutes of my life. And that afternoon, after he'd taken a ninety-minute-lunch with her, when I had asked him about it? He had only shrugged. *She's fun*, he had said. When I'd asked him if he liked her, he had cocked an eyebrow at me and questioned if we were all still in high school. Since then, I've kept my Chelsea questions to myself.

It's strange, seeing him in this role, seeing the tenderness come through all of the layers of playboy. How he sweeps a loose tendril of her hair and tucks it into her braid. How he lowers his head to listen to her words, and watches her when she walks through the room. I've had his undivided attention for so long—seeing it directed at another woman is disconcerting. I feel lost when I look at him and don't have his gaze, when I say something to him and it takes a moment to get his attention. I reach under the table and slide my hand into Stephen's, needing to feel something, a connection, filled with a sudden yearning to be held, cupped against a man's chest, the feel of arms wrapped around me. Stephen's arms, I remind myself, lifting my eyes from Trey's hand, from the slow slide of his index finger around the lip of his bread plate. I move my gaze up Trey's chest, his jacket open, his dark V-neck shirt snug to his body, light stubble across his neck and jaw. His lips twitch and I flip my gaze to his eyes. They study me, and there is a moment where I can't swallow, where a bit of bread just sits on my tongue. He slowly palms his glass, and I can only watch as he lifts it to his mouth. The simple act of sipping a drink shouldn't be seductive, it shouldn't make a woman clench her thighs or swallow in need. I'm suddenly thirsty, and hot, and I look away, reaching for my ice water, smiling when

Stephen glances my way.

Chelsea asks me something about my dress, and I answer, forcing myself to meet her eyes, to respond in kind, to have some stupid conversation about an episode of *The View*, one I haven't seen but that she seems desperate to chat about.

"We're going to Exuma at the end of the month," Trey cuts in smoothly. "You two should join us."

"They have wild pigs there," she says excitedly. "You can swim with them."

"Pigs?" I ask dubiously. "Is that sanitary?"

"They're very clean," she informs me, leaning forward, her voice dropping, as if this is a secret of some sort. "They have an Instagram account; I can send you the link." I don't tell her that I'm not on Instagram, or that I have little interest in swimming with an animal that I'm minutes away from eating. I simply nod, look for the waiter, and regret agreeing to this dinner to begin with.

"What do you think, Kate?" Trey settles back in his chair, and his foot bumps mine. "Exuma? You and Steve?"

"The end of the month?" I look up to the ceiling. "I think..." I look to Stephen for rescue. "Isn't that when we're going to your parents?"

He misses my cue but brightens up at the thought of me and his parents, an introduction he has been pushing for weeks. When he nods, I frown at Trey, painting my features with as much regret as I can muster. "Maybe next time," I say, and he holds my gaze for a moment before he turns to Stephen.

"Steve, Kate says that you're an oral surgeon."

"It's Stephen," I interrupt, irritated when Stephen waves off the nickname, his shoulders hunching forward as he launches into his spiel on tooth maintenance and root canal procedures. I glance at

Chelsea, who is studying her menu. I watch her hand leave one edge of the menu as she reaches under the table, my eyes zeroing in on a movement that has Trey pausing mid-sentence. She glances up, catches me watching, and colors slightly, her hand returning to the menu, the linen paper flipped over as she stares at the wines.

Maybe *that's* what it is. Maybe behind her blushes and soft words, she's a super freak. Something had to cause him to hop on the dating bandwagon after so many years of being single. I look at my own menu and try to push out the thought of what her hand encountered, what he feels like through his slacks, and if he had hardened under her touch. I flush and stare at the list of entrees. Yeah. We're definitely not going to Exuma. A full weekend with them would be pure hell.

"So, I've got to tell you, Steve." Trey sets down his glass and I sense the danger before he even reopens his mouth. "I've always wondered if Kate is as much of a hard ass in relationships as she is at the office."

"Oh please." I roll my eyes. "Ignore him, Stephen."

"No, really." Trey leans forward, his hands linking, his forearms resting on the linen tablecloth. "Is she an alpha?"

"I'm actually very submissive," I lie, for no reason whatsoever, except that Little Miss Chelsea here seems to be positively collared by design.

"Oh please," Trey scoffs. "You couldn't be submissive if your life depended on it."

"Put your hands on the counter. Flat. Palms down." I stare at him and wonder if he has forgotten that moment. "I think you're wrong."

"It's not a bad thing," he challenges. "A lot of men like a little fight in their woman." He glances at Stephen. "So settle it for us. In a relationship, is she dominant or submissive?"

He's asking a man who barely knows me, and he knows it. This isn't a question, this is a pop quiz, one to find out how involved my relationship actually is, how much of my heart this man has actually sampled. I rip off a piece of bread with my teeth and wonder how convincingly I can feign illness. Maybe we could skip the main course and escape after appetizers.

"She's not that simple," Stephen says, his hand running down my back, his fingers cool on the bare skin. "Just when I think she's the most independent woman in California, she'll surprise me." He leans in and presses a soft kiss on my shoulder. "Like you did last week." I flick my eyes up to him, a question in them. *Last week?* He leans in, lowering his voice. "In the elevator," he reminds me.

Oh. I wouldn't exactly call that a *submissive* moment; it was more of a weak one. The elevator in his building had shuddered, the lights flickering, and I had all but crawled into his arms, terrified of being stuck there, in the dark, a claustrophobic attack armed and ready. It hadn't been necessary. The lights had stayed on, and the elevator had resumed its climb, crisis averted. I shrug, ready to be done with the conversation. "You're right. I'm a paradox of contradictions." I stick my tongue out at Stephen, and he gives me that smile, the one he reserves for moments when he's enamored with me, and I'm not surprised when he leans forward, pressing a kiss to my lips. When I pull away, the waiter is finally here, and I smile at him in relief.

Him

The dinner is two hours of absolute agony, and I don't know if it had originally been Kate's idea or mine, but it needs to never ever happen again. Every time he touches her, my skin crawls. The prick kisses her, and I about come out of my chair. And I'll never be able to step on an elevator again without running through every possible scenario that could have occurred between them. The question had been a test, and he'd failed. Submissive and dominant aren't words that apply to Kate. She is both, constantly, and at the same time. She challenges me as she begs for domination. She argues for what she wants to be told. She needs a firm hand that gives her everything she wants. She needs me, and no one else.

Chelsea says something and I turn my head, nodding, willing her to go to the bedroom and sleep. Tonight was as cruel to her as it was to me. Each touch was a show, each whisper a power play, the entire meal a battle between Kate and me. Chelsea pulls on my hand and I stand, following her to the room.

"Wait here." She pushes me down in the chair, the one by the bedroom's fireplace, and I sink into the velvet, rubbing my hands across my face.

"Not tonight, Chels—"

"Shut up." She disappears into the bathroom, and I slouch in the chair, closing my eyes and resting my head on the back of the chair, listening to the sound of water running and drawers opening. When she reappears, I crack open an eye, her profile silhouetted by the bathroom's light. "Close your eyes," she whispers.

I don't, my head rolling to one side as I eye her, trying to understand what is different. It's her hair, it's dark and shorter, brushing the top of her shoulders. "What are you doing?"

"Shhh…" she says, straddling me. "Don't ask questions."

She leans forward, and it's then that I smell the perfume, the scent that Kate wears. I stiffen, and she lifts my hands, placing them on her hips. "Undress me."

"Chelsea…"

"Don't think about it. Pretend I'm her. You need it." She drags her fingers through my hair, and in the dark bedroom, with the dark hair, her smell … I can almost believe it. I can almost believe that this is Kate, and I can have her. Right now, I can unbutton her top and bury my face into her breasts. I can push her to the floor and have her mouth around my cock. I can carry her to my bed, and wrap her legs around my waist and tell her everything that I always think and never say. I love Chelsea for this, and I also hate her for seeing it, for how transparent I must be.

I drop my head forward, resting it on her chest, my arms stealing around her waist. I hug her to me and feel myself breaking, feel exactly how fragile every piece of my world is. "I can't," I say, the words gruff. "I'm sorry."

She leans back and lifts my chin. I'm glad it's dark, glad I can't see her face. "Don't be sorry. It was a stupid idea. A little creepy on my part, too."

I laugh, and drop my forehead into the crook of her neck. "It wasn't a terrible idea. I'm hard as a rock right now."

"Yeah, I can feel that." She rocks against me. "Any chance of me taking advantage of that?"

"Not tonight." I reach up and gently pull at her hair, the wig coming off, her blonde hair spilling out. "I'm in one hell of a mood. I'm just going to step in the shower, if you don't mind. Then I can take care of you."

"I'm fine." She rolls off my lap, bouncing to her feet. "I'm ten minutes away from a wine coma anyway." She wanders toward the light, and pauses, turning in the doorway. "But you're setting up something for this weekend, right? Someone for me to play with?"

"Yeah." I watch as she arches her back, skimming the dress over her shoulders and dropping it to the floor, the woman unable to resist putting on a show. This weekend would be her prime opportunity, me and two other men fucking her nine-ways-to-Sunday. I wait for the familiar pull of excitement, the high that precedes a meeting, but there is nothing, my funk still in full effect, my mind unable to pull itself off the image of Stephen leaning over, his face beaming at Kate as if she is his.

I can't keep this up. Something has to give, something has to crack. Otherwise, I am going to go mad. I'd think of a lingerie analogy, but my head hurts too much.

chapter 13
Her

"What do you think?" Trey flips the keys over in his hand and looks up at the chandelier, his eyes drifting over the living room's exposed beams before returning to me. Marks Lingerie just finished a record-breaking year and Trey seems intent on spending all of the profit. Yesterday, he cut me a bonus check with enough zeros to make Mom faint. Today, we are house-hunting. Not for me, but for him.

"I like it." I fall back on the leather couch, the giant cushion wide enough that I could do a mini snow angel of sorts. "Does the couch come with it?"

"Furniture is negotiable," the agent pipes in, her heels clicking rapidly across the wood floors, following Trey in the direction of the kitchen. I roll to the left, coming off the couch and standing.

"It's a little big," I remark. "Five bedrooms? Are you starting an orphanage?" I've dropped a few Chelsea questions, ones he has dodged with professional skill. A house seems like a significant step toward settling down. They've been dating six months now. Maybe they are getting serious, talking babies—this home the first step to their own octuplets reality show. Inside, the familiar burn of envy flares.

"What's that face for?" Trey stops before me. "What don't you like?"

I wipe the scowl from my face and try to come up with something, anything, to dislike. "The ceilings are really high," I manage.

He glances upward. "Yes they are. Excellent point. What would be ideal? Eight-foot?" He turns to the agent. "Can you put that on my requirement list?"

"Shut up," I snap, and the agent looks from him to me, confused. "It's fine." I turn around, looking through the giant windows and at the view. "It's perfect for you."

"It's got plenty of guest rooms," he points out. "I could use a roommate."

"Ha." I smile. "I don't think Chelsea would like that."

"Or Stephen," he points out, and I shift away, the conversation moving into the sort of direction we normally avoid. "Plus…" He turns to me. "You seem like you'd have trouble following the house rules."

"House rules?" I laugh. "Let me guess." He opens the sliding glass door and I step before him, into the backyard. Before us, a long pool glitters darkly, set off perfectly by the bright green grass. "Something about being naked."

He scowls in response, proof positive of my guessing ability. "And…" I muse. "Mandatory meal prep."

"It's not my fault I like your cooking," he says, offering a hand and helping me down the stairs and onto the pool deck.

We stop before the pool. "Want to test it out?" I grin at him and the edge of his mouth curves up.

"Ladies first," he beckons.

I anticipate his next move and twist left in the moment before his hand reaches out to push me in. Kicking off my sandals, I dodge another swipe of his hand, sprinting around the edge of the pool and awkwardly jumping over a lounge chair. He stops, his chest barely moving, and eyes me, his eyes alit with mischief.

"Don't even," I warn.

"What?" he shrugs. "It's hot out. And I'm dying to know how well my Creative Director swims."

I scoff. "Regional freestyle champion, 2001."

"Oh, I bet you blew those scrawny high-schoolers away," he drawls, and I laugh, easing further around the pool.

"Ummm…" the realtor stops in the back doorway, her worried eyes darting between us. "I don't think swimming is allowed."

"Kate," he lifts his chin to me. "Beat me across the length of this pool and I'll buy this house."

I laugh. "I don't care if you buy it." I'm perfectly happy with his current condo—and the gym it grants me access to. Plus, there's no way I'm stripping down to my underwear and getting wet, even if I *am* wearing our Crepe sports collection—the perfect accompaniment to any physical activity, should a woman feel inclined to spend three hundred dollars on a sports bra and panty set.

"Hmm…" he glances toward the house. "You're making my attempt to get you undressed really difficult, Kate."

I step off the pool deck and onto the grass before I make a mistake I will regret. Him stripping out of his clothes, me out of mine … he can call it a race, but we both know what it'd be—an excuse to see more of each other.

He tilts his head at me and I give mine a small shake.

He chuckles, and I can't help but laugh. I turn back to the house and look up at it. The pale stucco, the orange tile roof, the ivy climbing up its side. It's beautiful, worth every bit of its price tag. My favorite of the ones we've seen today.

He comes up beside me and hangs an arm around my shoulder, bringing me against him. "I like it." He looks up at the house.

"Me too. Can you afford it?"

He shrugs. "Keep the designs coming, and I'll buy you a matching one in five years."

"Ha." I rest my head against his shoulder. "And leave my apartment? Never."

I look up at the master bedroom, and imagine him at the window, fresh from a shower, a towel around his waist. I think of that giant kitchen, the tall fireplace, the view. I don't want a matching one. I want this one, with him in it. I want to swim naked in this pool and roll around in front of that fireplace, and make love in that kitchen.

The wind picks up, sweeping my hair across my face, and I feel, in the strong brush of its breeze, my daydreams scatter.

Him

I don't understand my cock. When I was younger, I wanted more kink. Something wilder than vanilla, something that led to orgies and threesomes, an audience often present during my fucking. Now, at the ripe old age of thirty-eight, I can only think of one woman. And she's not the one currently elbow deep in naked men.

I sigh, pushing open the glass sliding door and stepping out onto the Hollywood Hills balcony, resting my hands on the rail and looking down at the circular drive, one littered with expensive vehicles, a suited valet stepping from a Lambo and holding the door open to a couple, one who I saw earlier. From behind me, I hear the familiar shriek of Chelsea's orgasm, her sixth or seventh of the evening. It's a sound that should stir my cock, one that should, at the very least, pull my eyes toward the scene. But I don't care. Or maybe I do care, and that's the problem. Dating Chelsea has been my first experience with this world from the perspective of a couple and not as a single male. Being single, the situation was simple. I arrived, I pleased, I came, I left. Being emotionally involved with the woman in the threesome, or foursome, was a different scenario entirely. As it turns out, I don't like to share. There is something about another man putting his hand on my girlfriend that rubs me the wrong way. Chelsea said that makes me a hypocrite, seeing as that was how we met—me fucking her while her then-boyfriend watched. I don't think it makes me a hypocrite. I think different things turn on different people and, right now? Monogamy is looking pretty damn sexy. I don't want to deal with internet chatrooms and strangers and illicit meetings in hotel rooms. I want to memorize one woman's body and every sound and pleasure point she has. I want to please her in every room of my new house, and on every continent. I want to get married. And in all of those visions, Chelsea isn't present. In all of those thoughts, there is only Kate.

Kate, who is still with that tooth doctor. Kate, who gets flowers every other week, delivered to the damn office. Kate, who left for a weekend in Cabo and came back tan and glowing, her hair still curly from the salt air. It had been the longest weekend of my life, imagining what they were doing, imagining what he was saying to her. Chelsea had been a needed distraction that weekend. Hell, her presence is the only thing keeping me from looking like a lovesick idiot. And she understands, her breezy attitude about Kate almost annoying at times. What woman is okay with her boyfriend being in love with someone else? Maybe it is her generation, a younger attitude that accepts all circumstances. Or maybe she enjoys the expensive dinners and my cock. I turn, my back settling against the balcony rail, and watch her through the open curtains. On her hands and knees, she looks over her shoulder and laughs at something the man behind her says. Reaching forward, she looks up at the cock in front of her, her hand greedy in its grasp of it.

Ten years ago, maybe I'd have fallen in love with her. Now, I only want out. I pull back my sleeve and look at my watch. I'll give her another half hour of fun. Then, damn the situation, we're leaving.

chapter 14
Her

"So much for Paris in the springtime." I flick a piece of bread into the mist and watch a pigeon pounce on it.

"It's an off day." Trey sips his coffee and points down the street. "Look, the Eiffel Tower. That's all you really need to see. Now you can go home happy."

"Wet and happy," I grumble, scooting my chair closer to the table, its flimsy umbrella doing little to protect us from the rain. He chuckles and I wave my hand in the air to stop him. "Shush, I heard how it came out. Just get me somewhere warm and I'll be less grumpy."

"Fine." He stands, fishing into his pocket and pulling out some euros. Peeling off a few bills, he tucks them under the coffee cup and holds out his hand. "But we're going to have to make a run for it." I slip my hand in his, and he pulls me through the crowded street. My other hand pulls at the hood of my rain jacket, the downpour soaking my jeans, my flats squishing with water by the time he finds an empty alcove for us to duck into.

"Oh my God." I push the hood off my head and wipe underneath my bottom lashes with my fingertips. "I miss California."

He runs a rough hand through his hair and water splatters everywhere. "Don't forget, you're the one who wanted us to open a French boutique."

"It was a terrible idea," I decide. "You should fire me for it." I look out on the street. "I mean, look at these women. They aren't going to buy two-hundred-dollar panties."

"Maybe you're right." He leans against the wall and points to a man who holds an umbrella, helping a brunette across the street. "But he is. And so will the women, once that billboard goes up." He turns to me. "Or so you tell me."

The billboard is actually the side of a building, one that will host a ridiculously sexy picture of Trey, in his hottest suit, our LeCort bra hanging from the tip of his finger. It's part of the campaign I had brainstormed the night of Trey's mugging. This billboard was one of eight ads, all which featured Trey, domination pouring from the images. I had been right. He ordered women to buy our lingerie, and they responded in staggering numbers. Our focus groups had obsessed over it, and sales in US cities spiked everywhere we've run the ad. The billboard will be the first of a full French marketing campaign.

"It doesn't matter if they buy." I jump in place, watching my shoes, bits of water squirting out the top of them as I land. "This entire thing was really just an excuse for a free trip to Paris. And now that I'm here, and it's freaking bleak and dreary, I'd like to cancel it all. Let's just forget the grand opening altogether and fly home. I'll even give you a free grope mid-flight."

He makes a face, his hands tucking into his pockets. "No deal. I grope you anyway. As soon as you start drooling all over my shoulder, my hands get to working. But if you can wear a front-clasp bra, that would make my life easier. It's a bitch to undo it from the back, especially when people are watching."

I smile despite the weather and the hours of work ahead of us. He catches the movement and steps closer, his shoulder brushing mine as he matches my stance, both of us looking out into the street. Even through the rain and the fog, it does have a certain ethereal beauty to it. A beauty that I never thought I would experience and yet here I am, in the most romantic city on Earth, with him. I glance over, and he looks down at me, a grin stealing over his face. "You know we've done it, Kate. Pulled Marks Lingerie from the ashes."

I nod, and for once, I don't have words. Tomorrow, we will open the doors to a French store, a sister to the Los Angeles boutique we opened six months ago. This year, we will clear two million in profits. Next year, we should triple that, launch a men's line and five more boutiques. It's incredible what we've done, all in two-and-a-half years. As fucked up as our attraction occasionally gets, at least we have this. I've never been prouder of anything in my life.

I nod again, and he wraps his arm around me, his chin resting on my head. "Thank you, Kate."

I smile. "You're welcome."

"I love Paris!" I scream the words into the night, the wind carrying them down to the street, a few tourists cheering in response. An arm hooks around my waist, and I giggle as Trey hauls me off the balcony, his hands firm as he turns me in place and then points to the suite's couch.

"Sit, my drunk beauty."

"Yessir," I mock, plopping down on the red velvet, some of the champagne sloshing out of my flute. I take a small sip, watching as he feeds another log into the fireplace, bright orange embers curling through the air, some floating into the room. I close my eyes and stretch my bare feet toward the fire.

"Warm enough?" he asks, and the couch beside me dips from his weight. I roll my head to the side, smiling at the look of him, his bow tie loosened, tux jacket gone, the top buttons of his shirt undone. Rumpled. My rumpled and sexy man.

“I’m perfect.” I hold my champagne glass out to him. “Finish this please.”

He takes it from me and finishes off a hundred dollars’ worth of champagne in one thick gulp.

“Is it weird that I didn’t bring Stephen with me?”

He looks down into the empty champagne flute, then sets it on the side table, slouching down on the couch until his position matches mine. “No. It was a work trip.”

“Is it weird that I didn’t *want* to bring him?”

He turns his head to the side, his ear against the couch pillow. “A little.”

“Did you think about bringing Chelsea?” It’s been eight months, and I still struggle to say her name.

“It wouldn’t have made much sense to. We broke up last week.”

“What?” I readjust, turning slightly to see him better. “Why?” *They broke up?* My drunk self can’t handle the news; it doesn’t know how to react, and whether to cheer or cry. I’ve spent months trying to adjust to the impending possibility of their long-term relationship, months trying to see him as a friend and never ever anything else.

“You want the long or short answer?”

“Both.”

“She wasn’t you.”

Three simple words, yet they hit like sledgehammers. I look into his eyes and wonder how much of the emotion welling in me is from the champagne, how much is from Paris, and how much is from him. *I have a boyfriend.* I need to remember that. Stephen is a good and stable man. I just can’t, right this second, remember what makes him better than Trey. I swallow. "Is that the long or short answer?"

"The short one." He sighs. "The long one will have to wait for another night."

"I'm with Stephen."

"I didn't tell you that to change anything, Kate." He reaches over and tucks my hair behind my ear. "I was just answering your question. I wanted to try dating, I thought Chelsea would be a good fit." He shrugs. "She wasn't. It is as simple as that."

Would I be a good fit? It's a question I won't ask, a door I can't open—not when I'm with Stephen.

It's as simple as that. But nothing is ever simple, not when it involves the two of us.

Him

She falls asleep on the couch, her bare feet stretched out on the rug, her beaded dress bunched and twisted. I carry her to the bed, and she wakes enough to undress, my hand careful as I help her with the zipper, my eyes looking away as she peels the evening gown away, the barest of peeks revealing her choices for the evening—our Haviar shelf bra and matching eyelet panties, both pale lavender. I pull back the duvet and she rolls underneath it.

"Goodnight, Kate." I pull the blanket up and softly kiss her forehead. Moving toward the second bedroom, I stop in the doorway, looking back at her, dark hair spread over the pillowcase, arm limp over the top of the duvet.

Sometimes, I love her so much it hurts.

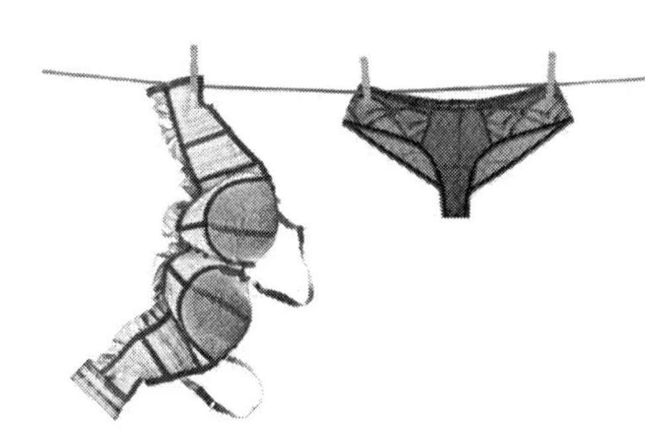

chapter 15
Her

“Please focus," I laugh, leaning back in the chair and rubbing my eyes. "We're going to be here all night if you keep getting distracted."

"Just try on the white one." He pulls a bathing suit out of the box and holds it up with one hand, the other hand wrapping around his beer, the bottle lifted to his lips as he grins at me. "Then we can go back to your comparison charts.”

The box before him is an order from Fredrick’s of Hollywood, and contains their entire summer lineup. We have ridiculed their products while finishing off an entire platter of tacos and … I eye the empty bottles littering the conference table ... two six-packs of Mexican beer. He shakes the flimsy white fabric at me and I snatch it from him, holding the ridiculous ensemble up by the straps. Its first downfall is the color—the type of cheap white that will turn dingy by the second wash. The second downfall—and the sadder of the two—the style. It has a poufy neckline, one that matches the little skirt that hugs the hips of the suit. I turn the suit around and am dismayed to see a *tail* of sorts, the skirt continuing in a manner the fashion designer had probably pitched as “seductive.” It’s a disaster. I toss it at his face and he tilts his head away, the swimsuit catching on his beer and hanging there for a moment.

He laughs and pulls it off. "Come on, Kate. We've been working too hard. I need some comic relief."

I snort, and lean back in the seat, kicking my bare feet up on the closest empty chair. "Nope."

"Try it on, and I'll let you have full control over the November catalog."

That bit of negotiation lifts my head. "Seriously?"

"Swear to God." He sets down his beer and leans forward, reaching out and sliding the garment toward me. "Come on. Show a drunk man how the competition looks."

I stand. "Don't test me. I'll do it."

He lifts his eyebrows in a challenge, and that's all I need, snatching the bathing suit off the table and walking toward the bathroom. "The November catalog. Full control?"

"You gotta sell it," he calls out. "Make me want to buy that thing!"

I don't bother looking in the mirror. I can feel the pooching of the material on my hips. My breasts are firmly supported by its stiff underwire, and the neckline is one that my Sunday school teacher would have approved of. I make sure that the tail of it isn't stuck somewhere it shouldn't be, then step out into the hall and head toward the conference room. Trey's dress shoes are up on the table and he turns at my approach, the chair swiveling under his weight, his eyebrows lifting as he sets down a fresh beer. "Well?"

I set my hands on my hips. "What do you think? Super sexy?"

He stands. "*Super* sexy." He nods to the window. "Go check yourself out."

At night, the sky outside dark, I can easily see myself, the way the fabric bloats around my curves in the most unattractive way possible—as if the designer had set out with the sole focus of making a woman look horrible. "Oh God." I cup a hand over my mouth and giggle, the combination of beer and exhaustion making the image hilarious.

I watch in the reflection as he comes closer, stopping behind me, his finger trailing up the side of my arm, his head dropping as he examines the shoulder of the suit. "Is this polyester?"

"It's a blend, I think. The tag's there, on the back." I reach back for it, and he bats away my hand, his fingers confidently dipping underneath the edge of it, his neck tilting back as he reads the tag. "You're right. Twenty lycra, twenty cotton. Though I'd bet..." He turns me toward him and looks down at the suit, his forehead wrinkling, deep in thought. When his gaze flips up to me, there is a twinkle in it. "Do you trust me?"

"Hardly," I snort out a laugh. "But yeah. Go ahead."

I jump when his hands settle on my hips, his body bending forward, his eyes on mine, and it is almost as if he is going to kiss me. I go to step back, and his fingers tighten. "Easy, Kate." he whispers. "Close your eyes. This is purely for research, I swear."

I shouldn't close my eyes, but I do. It's one of those senseless responses to a man I would trust with my life. I inhale when I feel heat against my right nipple, and I open my eyes and look down to see his mouth on the outside of the suit, his lips against the cheap fabric, his eyes closed. He suckles the fabric, and my eyelids drop from the sheer pleasure of it. Has a man *ever* kissed that part of me like this? His grip on my waist gets tighter, and I exhale as his mouth lifts off me. "What are you—?" The question falls away when he lowers his mouth to the other side, and I am unable to look away as his tongue swirls around the bead of my nipple, hard against the thin fabric. He covers the entire area with his mouth, and I almost groan with the sensation.

We can't do this. Trey's mouth on me, the bite of his fingers into my hips, my mind going crazy—pulled between lust and possibilities—he lifts away from me, and I struggle to open my eyes.

"Look at your reflection." There is a rough catch in his voice that is unfamiliar, and I look up into his face, unsure if I've ever heard it before. The heat in his eyes ... *that* I recognize, a look I always pretend to ignore, the connection between us that I always run from with a flippant comment, phone call, or eye roll. Now, I don't run. I stand, my heart wild in my chest, my nipples crying for more attention, and meet his eyes.

"Kate, look." His hands move to my shoulders, and he turns me to the window, his chest against my back, our eyes meeting in the glass reflection. When his gaze drops, so does mine, my cheeks heating when I see the dark stain of my nipples, clear as day through the wet fabric. "If I was at a party," he whispers, "and you stepped out of the pool wearing this..." His hands slide down the outside of my arms. "You'd ruin every man there for life." He tugs on the back of the suit's skirt, and the jerk of fabric pulls across my most sensitive places. "Even with a tail."

"Trey." I can't think of a distraction, can't think of a way to stop this. His eyes flick up, catching mine in the reflection.

"Is the crotch lined? I'm curious if it—"

"It's lined," I interrupt him, my cheeks heating, the thought of him continuing the test in between my legs … my knees almost buckle at the thought. "I should change." I want to grip the neck of his suit, just to keep myself upright. I want to rub the tips of my breasts against his suit, just to feel the friction. I *need* the friction. I almost lean into him, my hand reaching out, stopping myself just in time. I push gently on his suit and force myself to step back.

His eyes are on fire. I can *feel* the heat of his stare, it eats at my resolve and this is the closest we have ever been to breaking. "Be right back," I whisper.

His hand wraps around my wrist, tying me to him. "Don't stop for that pretty boy, Kate. He doesn't—"

"Don't." I flick my gaze up to his and all but beg him with my eyes. "You're drunk."

He says nothing, his eyes on me, as steady as the day he showed me his father's grave, as strong as when he gave me control of his company. Between our eyes, we fight and lose fifty wars. Then his lids fall over those dark eyes, and he carefully lets go of my wrist. "You're right. I am drunk." He turns away from me, ambling by the table and snagging his keys off the polished wood. "See you tomorrow, Kate," he calls, an exaggerated slur in his words. "I'm out for the night."

Him

I don't take the elevator all the way down. I stop on the sixth floor, moving quietly through the dark cubicles and into my office, my hand quick on the blinds, then the door's lock, my back hitting the door, hands fumbling at my belt, my zipper, my underwear.

Her hand flat against the window, cheek against the cool glass. I kneel behind her, my suited knees against the wood floor—

no.

I pull out my cock, and I widen my stance, clenching my thighs, my hand wrapping around my cock and slowly tugging down its length. It's half-hard already, and stiffens further under my touch, a soft groan tumbling out of my mouth as I picture pulling her from that window and scooping her up, knocking over beer bottles and lingerie and laying her out on the table. Would she fight? Protest? No. Not as soon as I lower my mouth back to that white bathing suit, my mouth teasing her through the fabric, lifting up her legs and wrapping them around my shoulders, her thighs against my ears, the smell and taste of her so close, right there. Fuck the lining of the suit—I'd get her so wet that I'd see it all, her all but naked on that table, the sight of her, her back arching against the hard surface, her hands reaching for me … I quicken my hand, squeezing the base of my dick as I jerk the shaft, my breath quickening, and I'm going to come like a fucking teenager for her.

I wouldn't be able to stop, I would pull her to the edge of that table and yank that wet suit to the side, exposing the beautiful look of her. She would be the first woman I would ever take without a condom, and that initial push, the thick slide of my cock inside of her, her name off my lips—

My shoulders shudder against the door, and I come, breathing her name into the empty office.

If my need was lingerie, it'd be blood-red, with lines that scream for attention.

chapter 16
Him

When the doorbell chimes, it echoes through the house, bouncing off wood floors and glass, the tones catching my attention in the moment before I reach for the remote. I stand, running a hand through my hair, scratching an itch on the back of my head. I pull at the bottom of my T-shirt, stepping out of the media room and jogging down the house's front staircase, the figure on my front porch manipulated by the poured glass. I hitch up my workout pants and pull open the door, blinking through the glare of the morning light. It takes a moment to recognize the man on my porch.

"Stephen?" Worry shoots through me, my thoughts rocketing to my last call with Kate, a few hours earlier. She'd been on her way to the store; we'd talked about increasing shipping costs and whether she needed a freaking parakeet. I should have told her to be careful, to get off the phone, to watch her surroundings and get back home. I—

"Everything is okay," he reassures me, reading the alarm on my face. "I just came by to talk to you."

As quickly as the panic came, wariness replaces it. I can count the conversations I've had with this man on one hand, all of them in the presence of Kate. There is no good reason for him to be at my home, on a Sunday morning, without her. I lean against the doorframe and cross my arms, sizing him up, my protective instincts on full alert. He's my size, but less fit, his frame less muscular, the sort that looks good in a tux but gaunt in a bathing suit. In a fight, I would demolish him—not that he would go toe-to-toe with me. He's too nice for that—too respectful, too friendly. He would adopt kittens but lacks the sharp edge to haul a woman to his side, then fuck her over the trunk of his car. My eyes move past him and to my new truck, its tailgate down, the vehicle blocking my garage, and the sleek collection of testosterone inside. I'd have her against its door, or sitting on that tailgate, her clothes ripping on its rivets and hinges, the cool metal against her skin, her hands trembling against its surfaces, her nails scratching its wax.

"I didn't mean to bother you." He clasps his hand, one palm over the other, and gives a nervous smile. "I'm sorry for not calling first. I…" he spreads his hands, "I'm running out of time."

Running out of time. I think of Marks Lingerie's fourth year, the two-million-dollar loan I secured with a trio of Italians who'd made my terms of repayment very clear. I had sweated through every minute of that year, through every check I'd written them, until their principal and interest had been paid in full. Maybe that's what this is about. My eyes flick to the nervous twitch of his gaze, and the possibility of his insolvency encourages me. "What do you need?" I ask.

He glances past my shoulder, hinting at his desire to be invited in. I don't move, my eyebrows raising, and wait for his response.

"Well." Those fucking hands spread again, and he looks at them as if they hold something, maybe the words that he needs. He looks back at me. "I know that Kate and you are close. Best friends."

Best friends. It's a title that should be reserved for teenage girls, not two people who can barely keep their hands off each other. My lip curls but I say nothing. Is this still about a loan? My body tenses at the idea that Kate may somehow be involved, that she might be in some danger as a result of his incapability to manage money. "Get to the point." I grit out the words, barely able to stop myself from reaching forward and yanking the damn message from his throat.

"Oh." He collects himself, then looks up. "Ah … I." He pauses, then starts over. "Tomorrow night, I'm planning to propose. There's an office party I am hosting—I'm going to do it afterward. Since her father is no longer living, I thought I would ask for your blessing. I mean, I know it's a bit outdated, but you're like a brother to her."

Like a brother to her

The rage ripples out, taking my thoughts and spewing them out, my words terse and deadly, barbs of truth that stab across the space. "I'm not *like a brother* to her. A brother wouldn't think about bending her over my desk every time she walks into my office. A *brother* wouldn't check out the curves of her ass every time she turns away."

The smile drops from his face. What an idiot. Does he not know her impact? The weight of her smile, her laugh, her challenge? Doesn't he understand that it's impossible to know her and not love her? His hands, those patty-cake-palms, clench into fists, and I hope to God he is about to swing at me.

"What the fuck did you just say?" The man steps forward, and I push off the doorway, coming to my full height and meeting his glare full-on.

"You heard me. Now get the fuck off my property before I embarrass you."

She will be mad. Hell, she'll be furious. But I'll be damned if anyone thinks I'm like a brother to her. *A brother.* My muscles tighten, and I come off the stoop and toward Stephen, pushing my shirt sleeves up, enjoying the rush of blood in my veins. A fight, that's what we need, the ability to take this back to caveman days and finish it. I clench my fists, and he steps back, his hands raising, his slick dress shoes moving down one step, then a second. He turns toward his Audi, his eyes warily staying on me. "I'm marrying her," he promises me, and the headlights of his car flash as he unlocks the doors.

"You're not marrying her," I disagree, and I stop, watching him nearly scurry around the hood of the car. "You won't even be engaged to her."

The words roll out confidently, but they aren't mine to give. I watch him peel out of my circular drive, his window coming down, one cowardly middle finger raised in my direction, and panic sweeps through me.

All Sunday, I wait for her call, for her car to screech through my driveway, for her scream to echo through my home. By Sunday night, I'm convinced he hasn't told her. By Monday afternoon, I'm almost at ease, my mind halfway through a clusterfuck of a marketing plan when my office door slams open, the handle punching a hole in the plaster, the artwork clattering against the wall.

"What the *fuck* is wrong with you?" I've never seen her so mad, her body literally shaking before me. I set down the folder and meet her eyes.

"Good afternoon, Kate. I was just reviewing—"

"Stop playing games and answer me."

"*Nothing* is *wrong* with me." I speak in the tone that would put a submissive to their knees. She doesn't even flinch.

"You told Stephen you wanted to *fuck* me?!"

"I do want to fuck you. I think we've all been clear on that for quite a while now."

She digs her fingers into her forehead, her eyes pinching shut. "I know you're not this stupid, Trey. I know you understand simple fucking society and how much what you just did severely fucks my relationship."

"You didn't have a relationship," I interrupt. "You had a guy who wanted a goddamn trophy wife. He came to my home and tried to tell me what *our* relationship is like. He told me that I am like a brother to you." I stand, and if this desk wasn't between us, I'd have her pressed so closely against me that she'd feel my need. "Do you think of me like a brother, Kate?"

She clenches her fists and looks away, as if there is a fucking answer in my potted plant. "I like working for you. I'm not prepared to leave Marks, but I can't—"

"I removed an idiot from an equation," I grit out. "Stop thinking about that and focus on my goddamn question. Do you think of me as a brother?" Fuck the desk. I walk around it and spin her to face me, pinning her back against the oak, my feet on either side of hers, my thighs hugging the rigid line of her legs. This close, I can feel her tremble. I pull up her chin and relish the fight in her eyes.

"I wouldn't want to kill my brother," she whispers.

"You wouldn't want to fuck him either," the words slip quietly out, and her eyes widen, just a hair, at their receipt. God, I am in love with this woman. The force of it yanks at my foundation. My hand softens at her chin and slides down the front of her sweater, coming to rest on her hips, my fingers biting into the fabric as I pull her against me. "Tell me you want to fuck me, Kate."

She shakes her head minutely. "I don't."

I lean forward, my lips gently brushing over her ear and down the hollows of her neck, my control wavering and I steal a kiss, just a few, along the way. I feel her shift in response, the work of her thighs against each other, the arch of her into me, her tells as loud as a scream. God, the things I could give her. The ways I could please her. I travel back along her neck and pause at her ear. "Tell me Kate. Give me this one fucking thing so I can go home, wrap my hand around my cock, and picture every filthy thing I want to do to you. Do you want to fuck me?"

She puts a hand on my chest, and I stop, the bite of my grip loosening, the breath in my throat stalling. I lift my mouth away from her ear and look into those eyes.

"You didn't have to say anything to him," she whispers. "I would have said no. It wasn't your fight. I'm not yours to fight over."

It should make me happy, but it feels like a breakup.

She steps back, and a part of me dies. "Wanting to fuck you has never been the problem."

I don't know how she can look into my eyes so calmly when she says it. I don't know how, when she turns and walks away, she doesn't stumble.

I watch her leave, and I've never felt so vulnerable, so lost.

If our relationship was lingerie, it'd be fur-lined handcuffs, latched around you, the key lost, escape impossible.

Her

When I broke up with Craig, it was clean and neat. With Stephen, our parting was rough, the result of a fight, one where he'd called me names and accused me of cheating, his face red, spittle flying. I had started out explaining, *trying* to explain the nature of my friendship with Trey, how he didn't mean what he'd said, how even if there had been moments of attraction it had never gone anywhere. All of those words had stopped in the face of complete hysteria—the kind, conservative man I'd dated for a year was gone, this new Stephen ripping a brass sconce out of the wall, then smashing a Queen Anne chair through the French doors. I'd shut my mouth and fled through the front door, all of my excuses and explanations worthless in the presence of that. I got in my car and ignored his calls, his voicemails full of venom and hatred, a combination that only cemented my decision.

Screw my attraction to Trey. Screw the inappropriate things he said. That night, I sent Stephen a short text breaking up with him for one reason: he was insane. Maybe his display of rage was out of love, a reckless passion he had hidden for the last twelve months. But it is unacceptable for him to behave that way, to handle *anything* that way, much less a few careless words Trey had tossed his way.

Trey is my new problem. When I'd left Stephen's house and went straight to the office, I was half-furious with Trey for causing it all, half-emotional from the fight with Stephen. Confronting Trey hadn't helped, his confident declarations catching me off guard, my system too raw to handle the dark look in his eyes, the soft touch of his lips against my throat, the brush of his fingertips and beg of his voice.

"Tell me you want to fuck me, Kate."

I close my eyes and wonder how I will ever face him again.

"You know you guys can't go back to being friends now." Jess digs out a bit of baby food and holds it out to Skylar, who clamps her mouth shut and looks away.

I sprinkle glitter over a line of glue and say nothing. *"Wanting to fuck you has never been the problem."* Had I actually said that? Had I told Trey that I wanted to fuck him? My mind hurts just thinking about the repercussions. I turn the cardboard page on its side and tap the excess glitter off, Jenna squealing with pleasure at the shimmery result. "He's in New York," I say. "So at least I don't have to see him this week."

"But you've talked to him."

"Yes." Of course we've talked. It's habit to call him on my morning drive in. Fifteen decisions a day go smoother when discussed with him. There is no "running of Marks Lingerie" without both of us, hand-in-hand, pushing it forward. "But on the phone … I don't know. It's different. It's easier."

"Because you can't rip each other's clothes off?" She gets up and moves to the fridge.

I eye Jenna's face, who blinks at me in the innocent way of a child. "Let's talk about it later."

Jess snorts. "Jenna, go upstairs and play." Jenna's chair squeaks against the tile and she is gone, her bright blue cowboy boots thudding across the kitchen and up the stairs with the thundering sound of a grown man. I watch Jess settle back in her chair, pulling the high chair closer.

"He flies back from New York on Tuesday afternoon," I say. "He wants me to come over for dinner, to catch up on everything he's missed."

Jess turns, her eyes wide. "Tell me you're going to finally do it. This is it! This is the moment!" She wipes off her hands and reaches for the house phone. "I'm going to call Mom."

"Stop." I grab the cordless handset off the table, tucking it in between my legs. "I'm not having sex with him. I'll be in Stage 9 period territory on Tuesday."

"Ugh." She gives up on her reach of the phone and turns back to Skylar. "Hey, maybe it's a good thing."

"It's a *great* thing." It's the only reason I agreed to come over. Nothing like a giant maxi pad to guarantee my virtue. "But it doesn't matter. He won't make a move." I don't mean for the words to come out glum, but they do. Every part of me, from my libido to my voice, is confused. Should I be happy? Mad? Worried? I pick up a colored pencil and draw a face on the page. Skinny nose. Cartoon eyes. Long lashes. I pick up a red pencil and hover above the blank space where a mouth should go. Finally, I draw a flat line, sketching lips around it that press together in a … I pull back the pencil and examine the sketch. *A constipated expression.* I sigh, and attempt to correct the lips into a smile, the ending result clownish.

"What makes you think he won't make a move?"

"He's had time to think about it. I think the Stephen conversation was a gut reaction for him, something he wasn't expecting and instinctively responded to. And then Stephen told me, and I came to him, and it sort of snowballed from there." I add a neck and jaw, then pick up a new pencil and add thick black hair. "When he comes back into town, he'll be back to normal. Under control." I say flatly.

"Which is … a good thing?" Jess asks. "I'm so confused by what you want."

"Yeah." I stare at the artwork critically. "Me too."

His Tuesday night flight is delayed, nixing our dinner plans. Wednesday, I suffer through two morning meetings, and finally connect with him in the conference room.

"You know, I did you a favor." Trey taps the model on the elbow. "Turn around please."

"Did me a favor?" I look up from the silk fabric in my hands, watching as he draws a careful line across the model's back, sketching out the lines of a bustier that he wants us to design. It's Wishful Wednesday, a monthly tradition on the second Wednesday of each month. We bring in a dozen models and all of the designers, giving everyone free reign with washable markers and a couple hundred material swatches. "With what?"

"Stephen. If it wasn't for me, you'd be sampling wedding cake right now and picking up his dry cleaning."

"I would not." I step beside him and eye the model. "That's too low. It won't stay up."

"But it looks sexy."

"It's not going to be functional."

"Tricia," he drawls. "Will you please get Kate in line? She's ruining all of my fun."

Tricia, the model I was working on, giggles. I glare at her. "Don't. You'll encourage him." I toss the robe to her. "Put that on for me."

"God, you're bossy." He looks up at the busty blonde before him. "No wonder they all request me."

"No one requests anyone," I gripe, wincing as he draws a criss-cross of straps that no woman will be able to get into without help. Tricia clicks her tongue at me and I try to refocus, grabbing a handful of straight pins and moving toward her.

"She was going to marry a boring asshole," he stage-whispers, and I smile despite myself, grateful that we are back to normal, as normal as the two of us can be.

"I wasn't going to marry the guy," I call out loudly, pulling the silk tight across her shoulders and examining the lay of it. "Now, please shut up and focus on your work."

"I'm done." His voice is in my ear, so close that I flinch, the straight pins almost poking Tricia, who gives me a worried look. He straightens with a mischievous smile, and I hurl one of the pins in his general direction. "Now stop wasting time and dream up something incredible. I'm going to go pick up lunch for everyone."

I try to glare at him, but I can't.

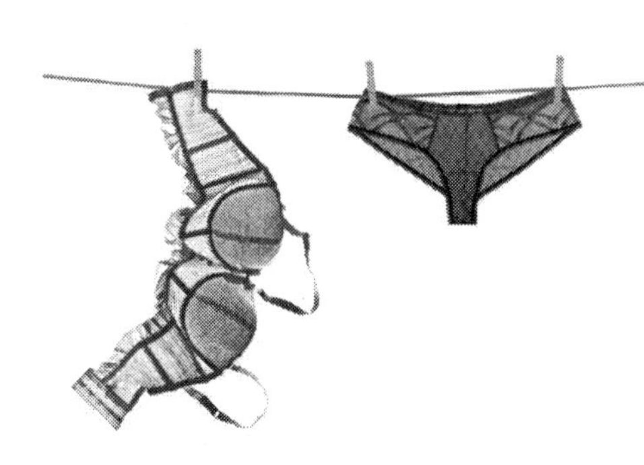

chapter 17
Her

I relax back in one of his chairs, my leg hanging over the arm, a blanket wrapped around my shoulders, and suck a bit of soy sauce off of one finger. On the coffee table before us, a sea of styrofoam containers sit, half-eaten sushi rolls and wasabi piles dotting the white canvases. "You ordered too much," I decide.

"The night's not over yet." He swipes a piece of salmon and stands, walking over to the window and peering out. "Want to go sit outside?"

"No." I stretch out my stomach, exhausted at just the thought of moving. "Entertain me from here."

"Hmmm…" He turns away from the window and raises one wicked eyebrow. "That sounds fun."

"No," I groan. "It doesn't. Entertain me verbally."

"Your French store is killing it. We should open a second location over there."

"No work talk." I sit up a little, inspiration hitting in the midst of sushi digestion. "Let's trade secrets. You tell me one of yours, and I'll tell you one of mine."

"You want me to tell you a secret?" He shrugs. "That's pretty open."

"No," I decide. "I don't want to know some stupid arrest you had in college. You have to answer a question." I narrow my eyes at him. "Truthfully."

"Oh please." He leans back, crossing his arms over his chest. "I'm not doing that. You'll ask about Mira."

"I promise I won't ask about Mira." I cross my fingers over my chest, and he rolls his eyes.

"You don't even have anything worth sharing. What's your biggest sin—borrowing a piece of gum without asking?"

I make a face at him. "You think you know everything, but you don't. I have all *sorts* of dark secrets." I wave my hands in a giant sweep, encompassing all of my many juicy secrets.

"Name one."

"If I do, then you'll answer my question?"

"As long as it's not a question about Mira. Or about us."

I turn my head and meet his stare. *Or about us.* We could sum up our entire relationship in those three words. Attraction. Avoidance. *There is an "us".* My heart quickens, that familiar race where I consider the *what ifs* that I typically try to ignore. "It won't be a question about Mira." I say slowly. "Or about us." I shrug, like I have no idea what I will ask, like the question isn't sitting, hot and ready, on my tongue. "I'll find something else to ask."

"And your secret has to be worthy." He leans forward. "Something scandalous."

I frown. "I'm not entering one of my secrets in some sort of Olympics. I'll pick a good secret. You'll have to trust me."

"*One* of your secrets?" He chuckles. "Kate. Please."

I glare at him, buying a moment while my mind frantically tries to find *something* scandalous in my history. I come up blank. My best secret is that I want my boss to strip me naked and pound me into next Tuesday. And I certainly can't share *that* secret. I think back to my college days and work forward, searching for something … my mind zeros in on the time I gave Victor Parken a blow job in the basement of his fraternity house. I search desperately for something, anything else.

"What is it?" Trey cocks a brow. "You think of something?"

"Not really." I pull at my lip. "It's personal." But look at what I'm about to ask him. *That's* personal. This—this was just a stupid night with too much Miller Lite and not enough common sense.

"Secret sex tape?" he guesses. "You strip in college to make extra money? Or maybe a secret baby somewhere? A—"

"STOP," I interrupt. "You're ruining my delivery."

"I'm sorry." He holds up his hands in surrender. "Confess away."

"When I was a sophomore in college," I begin. "There was a party—at a fraternity house." He straightens slightly, and I have his full attention. "I was drinking, and there was this guy I was kind of dating." His eyes change, growing wary, and I watch his jaw clench, almost imperceptibly. I speak quickly, before he thinks the wrong thing. "The party was getting crazy, and so Victor and I moved downstairs, to the basement." I pick at the edge of my sleeve. "We started kissing, and … I went down on him." I can feel the blush, hot on my cheeks, and I reluctantly look up to Trey.

"And…?" he all but demands.

"And what?"

"What happened?"

"Afterward?" I shrug. "I don't know. I guess we just went back upstairs."

There is a slow change to his face, a resettling of features, his handsome profile returning, and he rubs his fingers along his brow. "*That's* your secret? You gave a guy a blowjob?"

"In a *fraternity* house. And during a party," I explain. "Anyone could have come downstairs and interrupted—could have seen me." I flush, embarrassed at the thought. Me, my skirt riding up around my thighs, crouched and low on that sticky floor, one hand holding onto his hairy leg for balance. God, what if someone had come in and seen me, my lips wrapped around his—I clamp down the thought.

"But no one did come in." His lips flutter in the ghost of a smile.

"Oh my God. We were practically exhibitionists. If you can't see how stupid I was to do that, then you're—"

"Normal? Reasonable?"

"An idiot," I finish. "You're an idiot."

"That's not a secret."

"Are you kidding me?" I slam my hand down on the couch pillow. "That was a *great* secret."

"It's really sad if that is your best secret. Seriously. Tell me you have an orgy you're hiding behind that blush."

"Ew." I shudder. "No." I lift my chin and stare at him. "And don't belittle it. Just because I'm not a Trey-Marks-worthy-slut, doesn't mean that it wasn't a big deal to me."

"Oh, you're Trey-Marks-worthy." He grins, and we are back to that place, the one where he flirts, and I deflect, and later that night I spend twenty minutes with my vibrator.

"But not a slut."

He tilts his head as if considering the possibility. "In my mind, you are wildly promiscuous once out of those clothes."

"You're trying to distract me from my question."

"Oh yes. The dreaded question. Am I required to tell the truth?"

I give him a look, and he chuckles. "Fine. Go forth with this mysterious question."

"Who was that girl who mugged you? Why was she meeting you there?"

He grimaces, and I can tell he had forgotten that night, forgotten my tentative questions he had evaded. Back then, I hadn't felt comfortable enough to push for the truth, and had never brought it up again. But now, he has to tell me.

"That's not what you want to ask, Kate. Ask me something else."

"No," I insist. "This is what I want. I told you my embarrassing secret. You tell me this."

"I can't believe you even remember that."

"My boss stepped into my car in a bathrobe," I say dryly. "Your dick was practically hanging out of it."

Any other moment, he'd laugh. Now, he just runs his palms over his face. "Come on."

I wait, and he looks at me, his face so filled with dejection that I almost drop it all. I almost give him a free pass.

But I don't. I hold his eyes and wait for him to start.

"The woman in the hotel room…" he pauses. "She wasn't alone. A man was with her. I had scheduled to meet both of them." He looks up at me. "For sex."

I attempt to school my features, to contain the thoughts that come. "Both of them?"

"Yes. I wasn't going to fuck him; it wasn't about that. Both of us were going to please her."

"At the same time?"

He lifts one shoulder. "Possibly. Depending on how it went. Sometimes they just like to watch."

Sometimes they just like to watch. Will I ever forget how that sounds, the easy way it rolls off his tongue? I suddenly feel dirty, my desire to exit this conversation as strong as it had been to start it. This isn't what I wanted to hear. This isn't what I wanted to envision, not from him. I've known that Trey Marks has an active sex life. I've heard rumors, seen Mira and Chelsea, certainly never expected celibacy. But I also never expected this. *Sometimes they just like to watch.* My hands feel clammy, and I pinch the underside of my wrist in an attempt to fend off a sudden wave of lightheadedness.

"Kate?" He's watching me, and I look away, trying to hide my disgust. I run my fingers through my hair, everything suddenly hot. He swears and pushes off the wall, coming toward my chair. "Talk to me."

"Just a sec." I try to cough, to clear my throat and speak, but something like a sob comes out. I press my fingers to the edge of my eyes, attempting to stop the weak leak of tears. I regain some control and straighten, inhaling a deep breath. "I'm sorry." I exhale and feel a semblance of control. "I'm just emotional today. I don't know why I reacted that way."

But I do. This is major. Maybe this is the real reason why Trey has never moved past casual flirtation with me. Because he likes *that*, which I will never do. *Sometimes they just like to watch.* I meet his eyes, and the emotions in them are a combination I've never seen from him. Embarrassment. Sadness. Fear. He reaches for me and I flinch. He stops and stands, tucking his hands into his pockets and turning away, toward the window.

"So that's why you didn't know her. Or them," I correct. "They were just some random people off ... like Craigslist?" This is getting worse by the minute.

He doesn't turn to face me. "Christ, Kate. I'm not meeting people off Craigslist. I'm part of a club, one that pairs like-minded people and couples. There's a website where profiles are listed. I was in a bad mood that day and went off the rails, taking a risk on a new profile. It was a mistake, one that burned me." I can see the tension in his shoulders, the rigidity of his stance.

A club. Probably an expensive one, as if a membership fee and fancy website make it any less sleazy. *Sometimes they just like to watch.* I should leave. Walk away from this conversation, cross Trey Marks off of my heart forever, and move on. Never mind that I've spent almost three years pining over him. Never mind that when he breathes, I can feel it in my heart. He should have told me this. He should have told me this years ago, before I fell in love with him, before he injected his soul into my veins and I became addicted. Can I even work for him after this? Can I be around him without falling deeper in love? Before, I always thought there would be a time—once the company is kicking ass, once he is ready to step away from management and retire—when we would be able to date, when we could try a relationship. But now, with my one stupid question, with his one stupid confession, it all dies. I can't date a man who—I don't even understand what he does. I rub my temple. "Tell me exactly what happens."

"Kate." Just a single syllable, but I can hear so much in it. He turns away from the window and rests his back against the glass, his face hanging, as if he is a child being punished.

"Tell me Trey." I wait. "I need to know." I have to know how bad it is. He won't lie to me. He won't sugarcoat it.

"I enjoy pleasing women." His eyes lift and meet mine. "So that's what I do. With my hands and my mouth, and my cock. Sometimes the guy joins in, sometimes he doesn't."

"'Joins in.' Define it." My mouth is cottony. I swallow. It doesn't help.

"Sometimes double-penetration. Sometimes she sucks him while I fuck her. Or she jacks us both off at the same time."

"But you're not gay."

"No." He holds my eyes. "I'm definitely not gay."

Little difference that makes right now. I want to close my eyes, to look away, to yank at my hair and scream at him. I don't. I wait, and it's almost painful to do so.

"The woman is always the focus. That's the extent of my interaction with the men."

"Oh, that's it?" I laugh, a hard hack of a sound, one I've never heard from myself before, one that I instantly hate. His eyes harden, but he says nothing.

In that silence, I almost hear our future crackle and burn.

Him

I've lost her. I can see it in her eyes, in the tremble of her voice, in the questions that she asks. Maybe I should have lied. Maybe I should have muted the truth. Maybe then, she wouldn't be looking at me as if I am a monster, as if we don't have years between us, as if she doesn't love me at all.

I can't be surprised, not after that conversation so long ago, over beers and burgers, the disgusted look on her face when she told me about the threesome that her boyfriend had tried to have.

"Just because you don't understand it," I say, "don't judge me for it. We are all aroused in different ways. This is something I've done, something I liked."

She looks down, as if searching for a response. When she finally lifts her head, she blinks quickly, her face growing red. This stupid thing of mine is bringing her to tears. "You should have told me," she says tightly. "This changes everything between us."

The words are a hammer to the center of my chest. In them, there is everything that we've never said aloud, never put anywhere close to words. Is there an "us"? *Us* is more than I've ever hoped for. Between the risk to the company, and my sexual past, I've spent years avoiding any thought of *Us*. I always understood that we would, at some point, come to this. Her glaring at me, distrust thick in her eyes. Her flinching when I reach out to touch her.

Us. In a way, the word is almost freeing. The crack of the protective wall. Our rules gone, the battlefield wide open. "Us?" I tilt my head at her. "What *us*?" I step forward, ignoring her start, the way she peels away from me. "There is no *us*."

"You know what I mean," she whispers. "Our friendship."

"No, I don't think that's what you meant." I watch her mouth, the nervous way she licks her lips, her eyes darting from my mouth to my eyes. She's done it a hundred times before, the tensing for my kiss, the kiss that I have never delivered, but this time it is all wrong. It isn't breathless or hopeful. It is panicked and frustrated. It is … I straighten, stepping back, away from her. It is filled with disgust.

Incredible how quickly a world can change. How my entire person, our friendship, can be reduced to nothing, with just one confession. I've worried for years about her judging me for this. And now that it's happening, I'm as disappointed in her as I am mad at myself.

Is this who I fell in love with? A woman who would toss me aside so easily? Is she that judgmental, that close-minded? She isn't even asking the right questions. She isn't even giving me, giving *us*, a chance.

I turn away, my words tight and controlled when I allow them out.

"I love you, Kate. I am *in* love with you. I'm sorry that you don't like this. Or that you don't understand it. But it doesn't change who I am."

Her words stop me, their edges as sharp as broken glass. "Don't do that. Don't use those words right now, as you are walking away, you *fucking* coward."

I turn and regard her. My beautiful woman, the smartest woman I've ever known, the only person on Earth with the capacity to hurt me like this. "You're right, I should have told you a long time ago. But that wouldn't have changed this."

She swallows, her eyes wet, and says nothing. And this time, when I turn and walk away, she doesn't say anything to stop me.

I step into my bedroom and shut the door with a trembling hand. When she leaves, slamming the front door behind her, I can almost feel the vibration in my soul.

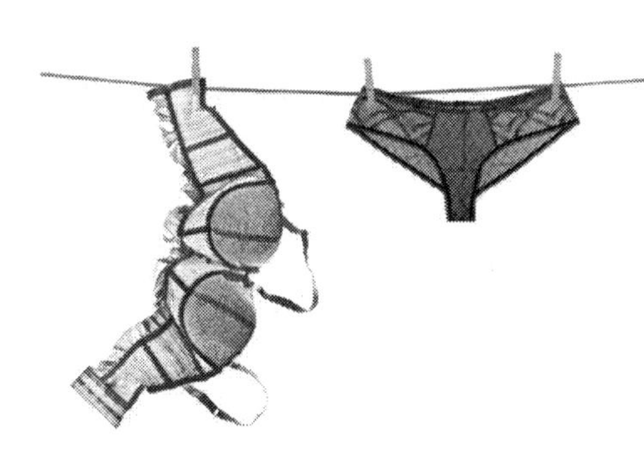

chapter 18
Her

We've fought before. We've screamed, we've sworn, we've said things that neither of us meant. But it's never been like this. It's never been this somber, this quiet. When he looks at me, all I see is sadness and disappointment in his eyes. When I look at him, all I can hear are his words.

Sometimes they just like to watch.

It doesn't change who I am.

He walks by, and I wait for him to turn his head, to glance in my office, but he doesn't.

"Harrods placed a new order."

"I saw it in your email this morning. It looks good."

"Trey, it's better than good. It's twice what they sold last month."

"I can do the math. I'm happy about it. Do you want a fucking gold star?"

"Don't be an asshole about it. I just thought it was worth mentioning."

"Is there anything else we need to discuss?"

Yeah. This. Us. Why we're suddenly strangers. I swallow. "No. That's it."

He stands, leaving his chair out, and pushes through the conference room door.

I don't understand why he is mad at me. I'm the one who is supposed to be mad, I'm the one who has been lied to for almost three years. I'm the one who fell in love with an unattainable man. I'm the one whose heart is breaking.

Part of me believes that. Part of me feels that I'm being a bitch right now.

Me: I'm sorry. I'm sorry for judging you.
Trey: I'm not accepting your apology via text. That's beneath us.
Me: well I'm not accepting your lack of apology at all.
Trey: that doesn't even make sense.
Me: you know what I mean.
Trey: come over.

Come over. It's been eight days since I walked out of his house. I stare at the phone for a long moment, then stand up and grab my purse.

Fifteen minutes later, when he opens his front door, I launch myself into his arms.

His chest is stiff, his body wooden, and I wrap my arms him, hugging my face to his chest, willing his stance to soften, his arms to move. When they do, when one hand settles gently on my hair, his other on my back, I almost cry in relief. He exhales, his breath warm against my neck, and he squeezes me tightly. "I'm sorry," I whisper.

"Me too." He pulls me inside and shuts the door.

It's barely cold enough outside, but he still builds a fire, and I make hot chocolate. We both finish and sit on the couch, our shoulders touching as we watch the fire. Trey peers into his coffee cup. "No marshmallows?"

"You were out." I rest my head on his shoulder. "I don't ever want to fight like that again."

"Deal." He holds out his mug and I clink my own against it. There is a moment of silence, his body shifting on the couch, before he speaks. "Talk to me."

"What do you want? Another apology?"

"I'm assuming you have questions."

"Some." *Some* is a bit of an understatement. I have piles, a list that is growing the more that I think about it, the more that I try to match the man I know with the fetish I don't.

"So ask." He sets his mug on the side table and reaches down, pulling my legs onto his lap, his fingers working at the laces of my boots. There is an unnatural tightness to his body, and as nervous as I am about discussing this, he seems worse.

"We don't have to talk about it. I know it's personal." I flex my toes as he pulls off the first boot, his chest brushing against my socked foot as he leans down and sets it on the floor.

He sits back up and moves to the next boot. "I want you to feel comfortable with it. I want us to be less…" He grimaces. "Less awkward about it."

"Okay." I watch as he frees my second foot. "Tell me about your first time. Like … did you always like that kind of thing?"

"My first time was when I was twenty-six. A bunch of us from work were out drinking. We drank too much, and my coworker offered for some of us to crash at her place." He glances at me. "It was Mira. And me." He pauses. "And this guy from the New York office."

"Mira?" I sit up straighter, and some of my hot chocolate almost sloshes over the rim.

He chuckles. "Yes. Mira. She all but stripped us both naked and dragged us into her bedroom. And when I saw him there, when I saw him touch her..." He pauses, looks at me. "There was just this moment of possessiveness. Like he was touching someone of mine. It was like I was suddenly in high school again, with my hormones raging and my need—like a ravenous need to compete, to win." He runs a hand slowly up my jeans, to my knee, and then back down again. "The guy didn't understand. He didn't get it. But Mira did. I remember her smiling at me as I fucked her. As he sat there with his dick in his hand. And at the end, she told me that she and I were going to have so much fun."

A piece of the puzzle fits together. "Wait. That night, in Vegas..."

"I met her *and* Edward," he confirmed.

"So Edward knew? She wasn't cheating on him?"

He nods, and I try to picture dignified Edward in a *threesome* with Mira and Trey. I shake my head. "You're full of shit."

His hand stills along the top of my wool socks. "Excuse me?"

"There's no way Edward would do anything like *that*."

His eyes darken. "Because it's disgusting."

Yeah. Disgusting is a *great* word for it. But probably not the best time to say that. "It's not disgusting," I hedge. "It's just ... kinky. And Edward wasn't like that." He wasn't. He was refined, and polite, and certainly wouldn't have had Trey fuck his wife, much less join in on it.

"I assure you, Edward is very much like that."

"But doesn't he get jealous?"

"He's a realist. He can't fuck Mira and go down on her at the same time. And he can't create the energy of two people, the attention of two people at once. With both of us, she has four hands, two mouths, two cocks." He slides his hands down, under my socks, and pulls them off. "I'm not an emotional player in their life. I come in, we have fun, and I leave. It's not messy. I get to please a woman, I release some sexual tension, and then I go back to life."

He runs pressure along the bottom of my soles, and I almost close my eyes from the feeling. "I don't understand." He sighs, and I look toward him. "I'm serious. Are you doing this for the testosterone-fueled rush or for no-strings sex? Because you know you can hire a woman for that, right?"

"Paying a woman to have sex with me doesn't turn me on in any way. And I don't know exactly why I did it. All I know is that the idea of it, the buildup, the unknown of a new woman, the forbidden-ness … it all turned me on. The secondary piece to it is that I love to please women. And this lifestyle allowed me to do it without requiring me to have a relationship of my own."

He's talking in past tense, and I register that, yet still forge on. "Except for Chelsea." God, I still dislike that woman. Even now, I can barely say her name without snarling.

"Ahh … Chelsea." He frowns. "Chelsea was an experiment of sorts."

"In monogamy?" So glad to know he failed that one.

"Actually, the opposite." He doesn't look at me, focusing on my feet, the gentle work of the muscles. God, if the lingerie business goes to shit, he could earn a million with just his hands. "I first met Chelsea in a threesome. I didn't see her again until her interview. Things didn't seem to have worked out with her last boyfriend. I thought that I would try the lifestyle from the other end. As a host, instead of a guest."

"And?"

He pulls a blanket over my feet and tucks in the fabric underneath them. "I didn't like it." He looks at me. "And it made me realize how I'd feel if it was someone I really cared about."

He's not talking about me. I *know* he's not talking about me but still, somewhere inside, a warm little flame lights. "Meaning what?" I say, in the most casual way a woman can ask a question.

He wraps his hands around my feet and brings them close to his chest, almost in the way that you would covet a tiny baby. "Meaning, if you and I ever date, I won't want to do anything like that with you."

Everything sort of stops. The crackle of the fire, the tightening of his hands, the movement of breath in my lungs.

"Ever?" I ask.

"Ever," he confirms.

"But wouldn't you miss it?"

"I can't watch you walk into a room without getting hard. I wouldn't need anything else." He rubs a hand over his face. "Honestly, if I had any additional stimulation, it'd probably be an embarrassingly short experience."

"That's a common problem, you know. That men have with me." I lift my mug to cover my smile. "It happens all the time."

He scowls. "Put down that mug."

"What?"

"Put it down."

I carefully set it on the side table. "What's wrong—" My question is cut off when he pulls me onto his lap, his hands firm on my hips, his eyes fierce with possession.

"I'm sorry I didn't tell you the truth. About Mira. About Chelsea. About my sex life. I didn't tell you the truth because I was worried I would lose any chance of us ever being together. And if I could go back to that first night, with Mira, I would. I would go back and never have stepped down that path. But I need to know if there is still a chance for us. If, knowing what you *now* know—and damn any risk to the company—if you will ever date me."

Date. It sounds so trivial compared to everything we've been through. Would I date him? God, I've been in love with him for years. I've—

"Jesus Christ, Kate. You're killing me."

I look down, into his face, my eyes traveling over the edge of his jaw, the tensing of his lips as he swallows, the lines of worry that mark his forehead and gather at the corners of his eyes. Our gaze meets, and everything I know is there. "I want more than that," I whisper.

I was going to continue, but I lose the words when he leans forward and captures my mouth with his.

Him

When a kiss waits for a thousand days, it erupts like a cyclone—a slow unfurling of lips, of tongues, hands ripping, clothes flying, hot swirls of breath met with a clash of frantic desire. I had always envisioned that I would take my time, that I would carefully taste her, my tongue sampling, a gentle moment that I would savor every second of. But in this kiss, we take a hundred seconds in every ten. I groan against her mouth and push her down onto my lap. Her knee moves, our hands fight to reconnect, then she is straddling me, and her hips grind down on me, and I break from her mouth just long enough to swear her name.

I've both feared and anticipated this moment for so long. I've wondered if we'd have chemistry or whether our tension was all a myth, the promise of the unattainable only hot because of its impossibility.

It wasn't a myth. I've never experienced chemistry like this, each taste of her tongue, each shift of her body, the yank of her hand in my hair—each one fans the flame, my cock pushing painfully against my zipper, my skin burning to have more of her, everywhere against me. I slide my hands down the back of her pants and grip her ass, rolling with her, until she falls back on the leather couch, her hair loose and wild, her eyes burning in a way I have never seen. I pause.

"What? What's wrong?" she asks, her chest heaving, cheeks flushed.

"Don't move," I whisper.

"You're not coming, are you?" Her eyes widen and God, I fucking love this woman.

"No." I grin. "I am definitely not coming. I just…" *I just want to savor this moment.* I just want to remember, forever, how she looks right now, the way she reaches for me, pants for me. I want to remember how her lips are swollen from my kiss, her heart is pounding, the glow of her skin. I swallow. "I just want to tell you that I love you."

She slides her hand under the waist of my jeans and grips my belt, pulling me down to her. "I love you too," she whispers, her mouth lifting to mine. "But right now, I really need you to get naked."

I can't argue with that. I steal another kiss as her fingers pull at my shirt, our mouths breaking apart as she pulls the cotton henley over my head. I stand and yank at my belt, nodding at her jeans. "Take those off."

I should take her to my bedroom, but that's too far away, and this moment feels like a mirage, one that could dissolve at any moment, her head in play, her doubts kicking, my past too much for her mind to overcome. I unbutton my jeans and push them to the floor, dropping to my knees as I move to the edge of the couch, my hands pulling on the waist of her jeans, helping to slide them down her legs, her back settling into the couch cushion as she watches me through heavy eyes.

I don't know what is under her shirt, but seeing the expensive thong as it is unveiled, the familiar style, knowing my name is against her skin—it does something to my heart. It's not just mine, it's ours, our labor of love, our late nights, our arguments, our passion. I spread her knees and settle in between her legs, my hands sliding up her thighs, toward the black triangle of lace. I run a reverent hand over the delicate material, tracing the details of it and then down, in between her beautiful legs. I lower my mouth to the lace and follow the path of my fingers, planting soft kisses from her hips to her mound, and I breathe in the scent of her, my tongue moving over the lines of the thong, teasing her through the fabric, a small whimper of pleasure coming from her as I hit her most sensitive places. She curves beneath me, and I hold her in place, supporting her up against my mouth, as I pull the thong aside and fully reveal her.

I've gone down on countless women. I've never tasted a woman I didn't enjoy, and I've never met a pussy that didn't make me hard. But Kate … I don't have words for the feelings I have when she is open before me, her thighs twisting nervously, the thin strip of her hair wet and matted with her juices, all of her exposed. I take a moment, my finger rubbing softly across her, and I look up, watching her mouth open as I gently roll the pad of my thumb over her clit, her body curving for more, her pelvis tilting, like an offering to the gods. I bend down and feast.

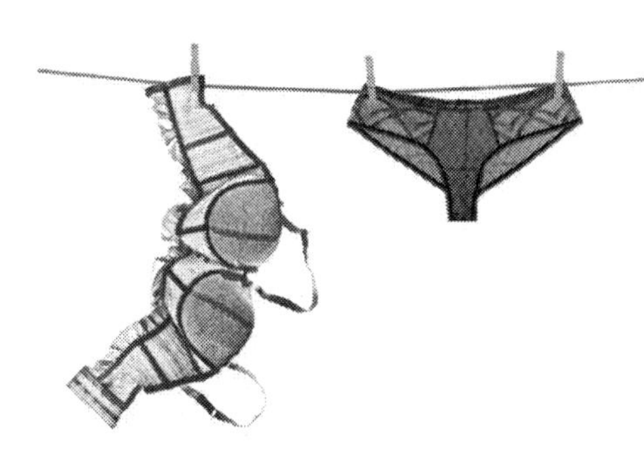

chapter 19
Her

The light from the fire makes him glow, a god with strong shoulders and muscular arms that pin me down as his gorgeous profile bends over me, worshiping my pussy with his tongue, his jaw flexing, the soft movement of his tongue tasting me in ways that are destroying my thoughts, my resolve, my sanity. God, all of the things I have envisioned, all of the talents I have imagined—every time that tongue peeked out of his mouth, every time I caught a glimpse of it—all my fantasies have fallen short to this, the look of him, the feel of him. He pushes his tongue inside of me and all thought stops, his fingers digging into the cheeks of my ass, his mouth as aggressive as his touch. I don't need to wonder how I taste, or if he is enjoying this. I close my eyes, release every inhibition, and let his tongue destroy my senses.

When I come, it is the kind of orgasm that changes lives. The kind where my nails scrape his scalp, my feet flex through the open air, and my scream is so loud it is silent. I scramble for footing, for reality, and in the hundredth call of his name, I tell him I love him.

He pulls me to the floor, my limbs loose and free, and I watch as he removes his underwear, his cock bobbing free.

Good Lord. And I thought he was sexy before.

I reach for him, and he lifts and positions me carefully on the floor. "Are you comfortable?" he asks, and I nod, his rug the impossibly soft type that you want to burrow into, one I have spent nights on before, but always in pajamas and never like this—never with the firelight flickering off his torso as he crawls above me, his mouth dropping to mine, and we kiss, this one different than the first, this one gentle and sweet, him tasting slightly of chocolate, each meeting of our tongues stirring my arousal, waking up my limbs, and I prop myself up on my elbows and reach for his neck, the drug of my orgasm wearing off, my body needing another hit.

Our tempo increases, layers of control shed as I tug at his head, our kiss deepening, his hips lowering. I wrap my legs around him, and a groan rumbles against my mouth, his bare cock hard against his stomach, and when he drags it over my damp panties, my sensitive clit, I gasp against his kiss. He pushes off his hands and sits back on his heels. In one quick movement, he grabs my legs and pulls me flush against his thighs, his hands reaching forward, and gripping the open neck of my flannel shirt, buttons popping and threads ripping.

A growl tears from his throat when he sees the matching balconet bra, the one from last season, his eyes scanning over my chest. He slides his palms up my stomach and over the swell of the sheer cups, all lace and underwire, his hands squeezing, fingers pulling at the top of it. "Fuck, you're beautiful," he breathes, and it is a moment of calm, a moment where his gaze drags over me, from knee to face, and our eyes meet and I've never felt so safe, so cherished, so beautiful. He swallows, and there is a catch to his words when he speaks. "I've always worn a condom. Every time. Always." His eyes drop, and I tighten my legs at the vulnerability that crosses his face. "But with you, I can't—I mean, I can, if it would make you—"

"I trust you." My eyes drop to his cock and I can't believe I'm actually seeing it, the most private piece of him, the beauty of its thick shaft, its lines and cuts, the twitch of it as I watch. I wet my lips. "Please. I need you."

He hisses out a breath and reaches down, moving aside my panties, my body lifting slightly off the floor, and I've never been so eager before, never been so needy for something in my life. I lift my body to meet his, and when he wraps his hand around the base of his cock, his eyes flick up to meet mine, a silent question coming from those dark depths. "I can't believe I'm about to do this." His voice is hoarse, and he swallows. "You have no idea how much I've thought about this." The hand on my panties moves, and my breath catches as something—his thumb—pushes inside. He swears, and suddenly, there is a break in his control, his hips thrusting forward, hand moving aside and I come up off the rug at the feel of him pushing, bare and thick, inside of me.

God, the slick, hard feel of him. The way he falls over me, his hands holding him up, breath jagged, hips pumping. He moves slowly, the first thrust difficult, the second easier, the third smooth and wet, a soft hiss leaving his mouth. I can feel his restraint, the careful way he slides above me, each stroke full and deep, then slow as he pulls out. Each movement gives me all of him, each retreat has my body craving. I claw at his back and beg him for more, and when he looks down into my face—I almost come apart.

It's *him*. It's Trey. It's his gorgeous face, that tight scowl when he is concentrating on something, the familiar burn in his eyes when he is aroused, the look I've always moved away from, always avoided. Now, it's more than a burn; it's a fire, his eyes devouring me, something so fiercely vulnerable in them, a look I recognize because I feel it—the terrifying realization that everything I've ever wanted is happening right *now*. Trey, my Trey, his mouth lowering to mine. His lips softly opening, his tongue against mine, my name a reverent whisper from his lips. His voice is thick when he tells me how incredibly fantastic I feel, when he tells me that he has wanted this for so long. Suddenly, he pauses, only the tip of him inside me, and my legs quake, and I curve my hips up for more, but he keeps me at bay, and there is the flash of his playful smile before it is gone, and he is all business, sitting back on his heels, his hand wrapping around the base of him as he pulls it out and gently, slowly, drags it over the top of me, my clit all but swooning from the slick feel of his head. "Tell me you love me," he commands.

"I love you." There is no hesitation in my words, only the hitch of breath right after, at the moment when he drops his cock and yanks at my panties, his strong hands shredding the fine lace, the ripping sound so raw and unrestrained, a slice of dirty pleasure sliding through me when he leaves the ruined fabric on my stomach. His hands move to my inner thighs, holding them open, holding *me* open, and he uses just his hips to guide the motion of his stiff shaft, his cock thrusting back and forth across the open spread of me, his grip keeping me in place, and I tremble at the hot, hard feel of him, slick from my juices, rolling with perfect pressure along my clit.

"Tell me that I am the only man for you." He lifts his head and meets my eyes.

"You are." It's true. He has been since the day I walked into his building, since I had to move my desk just to concentrate on my work. Since I broke up with Craig in Hong Kong, since my heart hammered in my chest when Stephen told me that Trey wanted to fuck me. He has been the only man for me since the moment he uttered my name.

"Do you know—" His hands tighten on my thighs, and I move up on my elbows, needing to be closer to him, needing to see the hard length of him against my skin, the way he pushes it along my slit, my lips spreading a little around him. He looks so impossibly big, so masculine, so thick and virile, his strong hands biting into the soft skin of my inner thighs, the hard ridges of his stomach as those muscular thighs flex. "Do you know how fucking *insane* it made me to see you date other men?"

I look up at the growl in his voice, a shiver of illicit pleasure shooting through me at the possession in his eyes. "Did it?" Oh, I know. I know how it felt when his lips had lowered to Chelsea's bare shoulder. I know how, when I'd straddled Stephen later that night, all I could think about was Trey's mouth against her ear, his hand under the table, our eyes meeting for a moment across a linen tablecloth and menus.

"I used to fake phone calls so that I could leave the room and be alone, get away from you." He quickens his hips, a swear rolling off his dirty mouth as he glances between our bodies for a moment, then looks back at me. "I would go into a bathroom stall and jack off my cock, imagining that you would follow me in there, and drop down on your knees." He pushes on my chest, and I move my elbows, lying back on the rug, my legs dropping as he moves up my body, his stiff cock bobbing over my bra, brushing against my throat, and then he is leaning over me, his cock at my mouth, and I open it, my tongue against the tip of it. I reach for it, and he grabs my hand with one of his and pulls it above my head. "Unclasp your bra and then give me your other hand," he orders, his eyes on mine.

I do as he says, and a rough exhale falls out of him as I undo the front closure on my bra, my fingers taking the extra moment to push the lace away from my breasts, exposing myself to him.

"Shit," he breathes, his eyes devouring the exposed skin. "God, Kate." His voice breaks, and I look past the bob of his cock to watch the muscles in his throat flex. "You're so fucking beautiful. I didn't even … God, I've thought about this so much, and I was still wrong. With how perfect you are." His eyes pinch shut and he lets out a long exhale, a shudder that ripples through his entire body. When he opens his eyes, his control is back, and he nods at my free hand. "Give me your hand. Up here, with the other."

I move my hand up, his wrapping around both of my wrists and pinning them to the rug, a change in position that arches my back off of the floor. His eyes dart once to my breasts, then he is kneeling over me, his other hand flat on the rug, keeping the pressure off my wrists, and I watch as the head of him moves before me. "Keep still and open that mouth, Kate."

I do, and he shifts, my eyes closing as he lines himself up, then the tip of him is between my lips, softly pushing, my tongue coming out to meet him, the gentle press of his hips pushing him deeper into my mouth. He moves slowly, a gentle dip in and out, his thickness not allowing too much depth, my efforts to take him bringing soft words of encouragement from his voice.

His movements get a little rougher, and there is a catch in his voice when he speaks again. "I used to fist my dick and think about you on your knees, your boyfriend back at the table, you apologizing to me with this perfect mouth. I thought about punishing you with my cock, making you gag on my dick, pushing it deeper, and coming down your throat. I wanted to send you back to him with the taste of me on your tongue, with your pussy wet. I imagined so many fucking dirty things, so many ways that I would punish you. You drove me mad, Kate."

He pulls his hips away, jerking out of my mouth, and I gasp for breath, my thighs twisting together, the need between them too great. My orgasm from his mouth seems hours ago, and I need something, anything, to rub against, to penetrate. "Please," I beg. "Fuck me."

He chuckles, and pushes off the rug, releasing my hands and sitting up above me, my saliva dripping off him, and his eyes flare with arousal as he takes a moment to drag the head of him over my lips. "You are going to be the death of me."

I lift my upper body, and my breasts brush against his ass, his knees still on either side of my shoulders. "Fuck me," I demand.

His smile grows wider. "Are you sure you want that? For me to well and truly fuck you?"

I recognize a Trey Marks challenge when I hear one. In three years, there have been many. Most, I have approached with a cautious hand. This one, I grab by the fucking balls. Or rather, by the shaft. I grip my hand around him and squeeze, and the shock of it all is still there. *I am touching Trey's cock.*

He gives one short thrust against my palm, then jerks to his feet, holding out a hand and helping me up. "Put your knees on the couch, hands on the back of it." The words are hard and business-like, the kind that don't allow for discussion, and I scramble, my skin hot from the fire, the leather cool as it yields to the pressure of my knees, my hands gripping the back cushion. I hear the slide and collide of metal, and turn to see Trey, bare-assed in front of the windows, raising and locking them into place, a cool breeze immediately entering the room and fighting with the warmth from the fire. "Not there," he snaps, pointing to the end of the sectional, the one closest to the fire. "Here."

I move closer, and when I get back on my knees and tilt forward, I look over my shoulder at him. He's a dark silhouette before the fire, an outline of raw sexuality, of strong arms and hips, of hard ass and abs. He strokes himself and comes forward, and there is a moment of reverence when his hands close over each of my ass cheeks. "Are you holding on to the couch?" he asks.

"Yes." God, I want this. I want him to be raw and rough. He shoves inside of me, and it's an invasion. There are no slow and controlled strokes, no gentle draws to allow my body to adjust. This is straight fucking, and it is exactly how I'd always pictured Trey would do it—wild and furious, the bite of his fingernails into my skin, the slam of his thick cock in and out, the grunt of him, the slap of our thighs, the moment when he reaches forward, his hands jerking at the bra that still hangs from my shoulders. "Keep your hands on the couch," he grits out, and he grips one of my shoulders, using it for leverage, as if I am a wild stallion that he is taming. It takes only seconds for me to come, for the last twenty minutes of teasing to erupt into one overwhelming shatter of senses. I claw at the leather, I scream his name, and when my entire body tenses, it is a rolling, tumbling fall of ecstasy that doesn't stop, the animalistic sounds coming from him, the continual mad thrusts of his body, the jerk of the lace, the assault of cock and balls against and inside of me … I scream over and over, and if this is a Trey Marks orgasm, I am ruined for life. I cannot, will not, ever find this again. I cannot, will not, ever experience this again. There is no way that a body can feel this good, can come apart this completely, and survive. I hover in some plane, some beautiful place where it doesn't end, where he and I are fully connected, every line of our bodies intact. When I come back to life, it is with a shudder, my arms falling from the couch, my body pitching forward, and when my cheek hits the couch, I open my eyes.

Fire glowing, its shape blurry, my eyes tearing. Cool air against my skin, yet I'm warm everywhere, his body thrusting, the slap of us together like a chant in the room. He is saying something, something about me, something about love and fucking and how I feel. He is sliding his hands down my arms, pulling my wrists together at the small of my back, and then they are being bound by his grip, a tight hold while he continues, while he thrusts and pulls, and I don't think I've ever been so wet, so warm, so oblivious to everything but the moment where we connect, the thick feel of him inside of me, the fill and then empty, perfection and then need. He moves me to the side, where my head has more room against the seat of the couch, and I feel everything shift as he climbs onto the leather, my ass up in the air, hands still held behind my back. He pushes back inside and the feeling is different, the angle new, the pleasure a twisted blend of something else, and any coherent thought is gone as he leans forward, one hand playing over my nipples. These thrusts are slower, deeper, more intense. He squeezes my breasts and I tell him he is a god. He pulls on them gently, rubs his fingers over their curves and he tells me how much he loves me.

Then, his hands release my wrists and the pace picks up.

At some point, I am against the last window, the tall pane of glass that doesn't open, my bare breasts against the cold surface, my cheek pressed to it, his hand knotted in my hair, holding me in place. The other is at my hip, and he moves fluidly and perfectly, not all of the way in, just little notches of pleasure that drive me to another orgasm, one where my legs collapse and he carries me to the floor, lying me on my back.

"I'm going to come," he pants out, almost apologetically, as if his performance is weak, and this is his third thrust, and he just can't control himself. "Where do you want it?"

"Inside of me."

"Fuck, I'm glad you said that." His tempo increases, and when he comes, he says my name in a way that is almost a prayer, his breaths ragged, his eyes on me. When he gives a final shuddering push, I wrap my arms around him and whisper out everything I've never said. How much I love him. How much I've needed him. How much, in the middle of the day, in the middle of the night, for our entire friendship, I've wanted him.

He falls onto the rug and pulls me on top of him. "Tell me you'll stay with me. Tell me this is forever."

"It is." I lift my head off his chest and look into his eyes. Inside, a part of me worries. Inside, a part of me is terrified. But when I look into his eyes, when I see the man I know, it all goes away.

There are few things I know in life. But I know that look in his eyes. I know when he is committed to something, when he is making a promise that he will fight with every bit of his soul to keep. He has that look when it comes to his company, the one he's risking for us. And this look is even stronger. This look is one dipped in love.

He swallows, his jaw tightening, his throat moving, and his eyes change, just a little, before he speaks.

"Marry me," he says, and for such a strong man, there is so much vulnerability in those vowels.

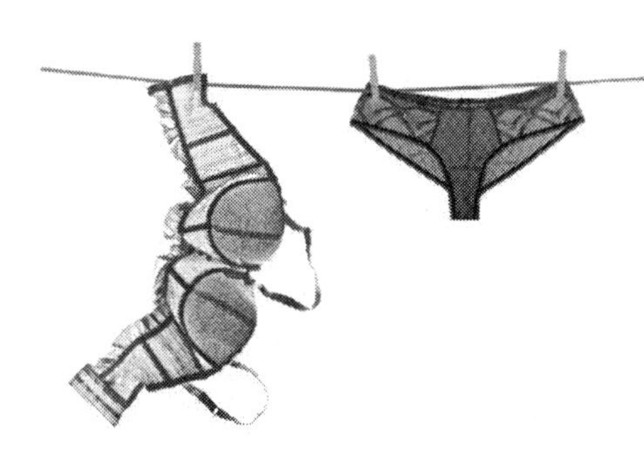

chapter 20
Him

I don't know where the words come from. They fall out of my mouth and hang between us, and damn if I never want to put them back in.

Marriage is something I stopped thinking about a long time ago, around the first time I had a husband ask me to screw his wife. Monogamy just didn't seem to be that sacred a concept, the thought of freedom more tantalizing. But then I met her—I fell for her. An hour ago, I was afraid to bring up dating, afraid at the risk I was bringing to my company and our friendship. That was just an hour ago. And now, a proposal? It's too quick, ridiculously too quick. I'm going to scare her off, going to ruin everything. Her loving me isn't the same as a commitment that will bind us—

"Trey." She touches my face, her fingers soft, and it's over. You don't respond to a marriage proposal with a name. I close my eyes and can feel the hopelessness when it hits, the down that comes after a high. Her lips brush against mine, her nails soft against my cheeks, the tickle of her hair as it falls against my ear.

"Ignore that," I mumble. "It was stupid." I need to recover. I need to open my eyes, and make a dirty remark, and give her that smirk—the one that gets me out of trouble and covers mistakes. I need to do all of it, but can't muster up a smile, can't come back to life after drowning.

"Don't say that."

"It was."

"I *want* to marry you."

I take a risk and look up at her, the fire's light playing across her features, and there is a *but* coming, I can feel it pushing off her tongue. "But," she says, and then her eyes drop, her fingers running over my bottom lip. I open my mouth and gently bite down on her thumb. Her eyes flick back to mine. "But, I'm worried about the orgy stuff."

It is so unexpected, that I can't help but smile. She scowls in response, and I know suddenly that we will be fine, that we are Kate and Trey, and even if we don't marry, there is nothing that can come between us. "It's not funny," she says, pushing on my chest.

"The orgy stuff?" I repeat, and I try to contain my smile, to take seriously whatever is about to come out of her delicious mouth.

"Yes, Trey. The orgy stuff." She huffs out a breath, sitting upright.

I can't stop the laugh that comes at her petulant expression. "I don't do orgies, Kate." I quickly amend the words. "I haven't *done* orgies. I was only the third for couples. That's it."

"Okay, sorry. The *threesome* stuff." She rolls her eyes. "Is that better?"

"Yes." I slide my hands up her bare thighs, and I like this position, having her astride me, her pussy bare on my stomach, wet from my come, her hair falling over her breasts, her face flushed from our sex and her current indignation over my pain-in-the-ass past. "What worries you about it?"

"I'm just worried that you'll want me to do that. And it's not that I'm a prude or anything—"

I pop my hips enough that she bounces up, and she stops talking, caught off balance, her hand reaching out to stabilize herself as she comes back down to my stomach, my hand taking advantage of the moment to slip underneath her. I slide two fingers inside, curving them up and toward me, and her objection dies as she melts forward. "Trey," she protests, and it is a weak slur of my name, my fingers gently sweeping over her g-spot, and she is so warm, so tight, so wet inside. I wonder how much of it is my come, and how much is her, and how, if I press right *there* … she curses and digs her fingers into my chest.

"Jesus, Trey. Don't stop."

"Look at me, Kate."

My confidence rises when she tries to lift her eyes to mine. They are heavy, her eyes hooded and glazed, and thank God I am only now discovering this—how responsive she is to just the crook of my finger. If I'd known this early on, I'd have solved every business discussion this way. I'd have insisted that she only wear skirts to work. I would have installed a wall of mirrors in my office and have her face them, have her watch her face as I fingered her, have her see exactly how motherfucking sexy she looks like this. I sweep my thumb over her clit and use my fingers in short thrusts, making sure to brush over that spot, her mouth falling open, short pants leaving it, her hips beginning to rock over me.

"I will never want to share you with anyone." I promise her, my eyes on her face, a jolt of pleasure coming through me as she squeezes her eyes shut, a low moan leaving her. I slow my motions. "Tell me you understand."

"Don't stop," she begs, her hand clawing at my chest. "I understand."

"I will never want another woman. Ever." I resume the manipulation of my fingers and she tightens, the walls of her flexing around my fingers, her g-spot swelling. "There is not another woman who can ever compare to you." She stiffens, her head dropping back, her neck exposed, and it takes all of my control to stay in place, to keep my fingers' cadence. I use my other hand and run my palm over her bare breasts, vowing to spend all day tomorrow focused on them, dedicated to my worship of their perfect flesh. Her nipples tighten under my caress, and I bite my lips, the desire to suck them into my mouth almost impossible to resist.

I don't know how to convince her, how to tell her that what we just shared was a hundred times better than any sexual experience I've ever had. I don't know how to explain that just the sound of her voice awakens my cock more than a hundred threesomes ever could. I don't know how to tell her that the thought of sharing her twists my gut in the most painful way.

"Do you understand?" I stop her orgasm in the breath before it comes, my fingers wilting, my voice strong enough to cause her eyes to flip open, and she grounds her hips on top of my hand, shamelessly trying to maintain my rhythm.

"Yes," she gasps. "I understand."

"Tell me you'll marry me," I order. "No buts."

She purses her lips and the hint of a dimple appears in her cheek. "You're trying to negotiate marriage over an orgasm?"

I push both fingers into her, cupping them, and watch the blur of her focus. "Yes, Kate. That's exactly what I'm doing."

She gasps, and her hips lift off me as I increase the speed and depths of my movements, finger-fucking her toward the orgasm she wants, her mouth spreading into a smile as she grabs ahold of my other hand, holding it over her breast, her fingers squeezing mine into a grip, her flesh swelling through our fingers. "Yes," she whispers, her eyes meeting mine, and I jerk my fingers out of her, my wet hand gripping her hip and pushing her back, my cock hard and waiting, the moment when I push her down on it—

It's the most beautiful moment of my life.

Her eyes close, and she breathes out my name, her body shuddering around mine, and I pull her to my chest, holding her in place as my hips hammer upward—short, quick strokes that slap my pelvis against her clit and bury my cock into her heat, her inner walls tightening, then flexing, and when she comes, I can feel it rip through her entire body, her cry of my name more animal than human. She screams the word *yes*, first quick and shrill, then louder and longer, my movements not slowing, not easing, my control shredding as she gives me everything I want.

When I come, it feels as if it lasts a minute, and if she ever stopped coming, I couldn't tell. I give one last, deep thrust and then hold her against me, my cock twitching as the aftershocks tremble through me.

I close my eyes, and I can't stop the goofy smile from stretching over my face. I don't know if she meant the proposal acceptance, but I've never been happier in my life.

In this one moment, everything is perfect.

Her

I think he's dead. He's stretched out, stark ass naked, his eyes closed, a limp smile on that gorgeous face. His cock is lying across his stomach, and if sucking it will bring him back to life, I'll be the first volunteer. I smile at the thought and roll off him, pushing to my feet and making my way to the windows, my limbs loose and lazy, my knees almost buckling as I reach up and grip the top of the window.

"I'll do that," he mumbles, his head moving, one eye opening to watch me. I bend over and slide the first one closed, and the corner of his mouth lifts up. "Never mind," he muses. "You do it much better. Especially naked like that."

"Shut up." I close the other two and return to him, stepping over his chest and stopping, extending my hand. "Come on. We both need showers."

"You're evil," he groans, his eyes between my legs. "I thought you looked good in my lingerie but *fuck*." He drawls out the last word, his eyes shameless in their perusal. "I'd rather you work naked."

"That won't work." I wave my hand impatiently in front of him. "My fiancé is a jealous bastard. He doesn't like it when other men look at me."

It's as if I've given him a gift. His eyes lift to my face, and his lips twitch into a new smile, a shy one. "I think he likes it when they look. He just doesn't like it when they touch." He finally takes my hand, his legs coming up underneath him, and I lift my chin to look up into his face when he stands.

"Is that so?" I say.

"I wouldn't blame any man for ever looking at you, Kate," he says softly. "You're the most beautiful woman any of us have ever seen."

"You're so full of shit." I smile.

His hands come up, and he holds my face, his eyes deepening as he looks into mine. "Tell me more about your fiancé."

"Hmm." I muse. "He's very smart. Almost annoyingly so. And he knows it, which makes it even worse. And he's cocky. But in that confident, sexy way that makes you want him to rip off your clothes as soon as you meet him. But he's also unbelievably sweet." He presses his lips to mine, just a gentle pull of love, and then a release, his eyebrows raising for more. "And generous," I add, earning a second kiss. "And…" I scrunch my brow, as if I am thinking hard for another compliment. *And kind. And funny, and loving, and vulnerable, and witty, and intoxicating, and every positive word that Webster ever created.*

"Addictive?" he supplies.

I twist my lips. "Kind of." I venture. "I'm not sure yet. It's a fairly new engagement."

"Do you think it will stick?" His hands tighten, and he draws me closer.

I look up into his eyes. "I do. I want it to."

"It will." He lowers his mouth, and this kiss—it is more of a promise, the sort that wipes away all doubt and tells me a thousand times over, with each brush of his lips, that he means this. That we will stick, that all of *this* will last.

He lifts his mouth from mine. "I love you."

"I love you too."

I pull the blanket back and crawl under the sheets, the act almost reverent in its execution. I've never been in his bed with him, never slid, bare skin to bare skin, against his body. He had insisted on my sleepwear—a sheer slip from last season, and he wraps a hand around me, pulling me across the king bed and against him, my bottom snug to the bend of his body, his hand closing possessively over one breast. I relax against the pillow, my eyes picking up all of the details before me. The closed curtains, their edges framed in soft moonlight. The glow from the bathroom's nightlight giving subtle definition to the art, the dark blue walls, the elephant lamp on the bedside table. His breath is warm against my neck, and he squeezes me gently, just a test, as if to see if I am still here. I cup my hand over his and lower my mouth to his fingers, one kiss pressed against the digits.

In the morning, maybe all this will be gone. In the morning, we both might regret everything.

I stay awake as long as I can, enjoy as much as I can, the feel of him, the sounds of him sleeping. In the quiet room, I whisper my love for him.

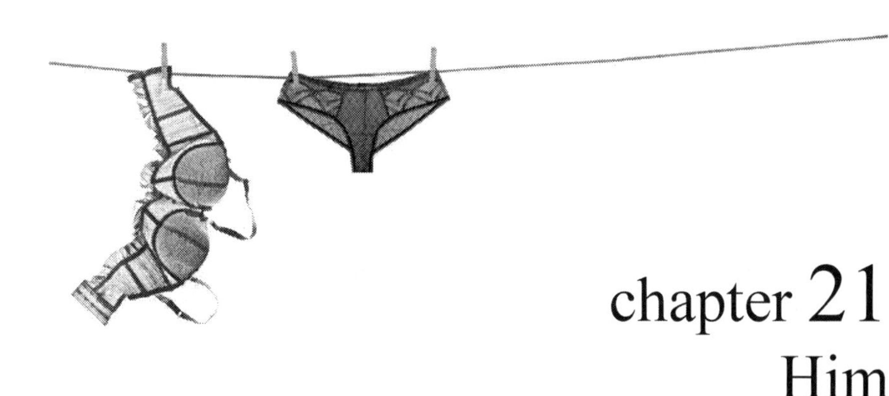

chapter 21
Him

"It feels weird," I confess, sliding a box of cereal toward her. "Being able to do the things I've thought about for so long."

"I know." She smiles, opening the top of the cereal box. "I feel the same. Like I'm cheating or something."

"Should I have done this sooner?" I ask, leaning my forearms on the counter and watching her, the fall of her dark hair as she looks down, watching the frosted Cheerios fall into the bowl. "Made a move on you?" God, the wasted years. All of the trips we've made, the late nights we've worked, the times I'd locked myself in my office and jacked off, thinking of her lips around my cock, her body in my hands.

"I don't know," she says, considering the thought. "I'm not sure we would have worked out if we had tried to date earlier." She uncaps the milk and lifts it, pouring into the bowl. "Like … after I broke up with Craig?" Her eyes meet mine as she sets the jug back down. "I feel like our relationship was so weak back then. I mean, compared to how we are now. There was attraction … but I don't know if it would have lasted."

I scowl at the idea of us ever *not* making it, even if in a fictional scenario.

"Plus, you hadn't dated Chelsea," she points out. "You probably would have tried to get me in some kind of kinky ninesome."

I make my way around the island, hating even the idea of it. "I told you, you don't have to worry about that."

"I know, but I'm just pointing out that Chelsea helped with that. Just like Stephen helped me to see one version of a relationship, and Craig helped me to see a different one." She scoops a spoonful of cereal and brings it to her mouth, her lips parting for the silver utensil, my dick hardening at just the tiny glimpse I get of her tongue. I want to hop up on the counter right now. Slide her stool over until it is before me, my legs hanging before her, her hand digging into my thighs, her feet bare against the stool's rungs. She chews, her jaw moving, and I think about how hard she had tried to take all of me, her eyes moving to mine, that jaw stretching, the play of her tongue against my shaft, the—

"Trey." Her lips part around the word, and I am off of my stool and pulling her against me, the spoon clattering against the tile floor, her arms wrapping around my neck, and she tastes like sugar and milk, her mouth as greedy as mine, her body light when I lift her up and onto the counter. The reality is better than my fantasy, her panties easily skimmed off, her knees parting, and I pull my mouth from her kiss and move down, to the only thing better.

chapter 22
Her

five months later

I close my eyes and rub my forehead, glancing at my watch, the minutes passing interminably slow. Over the phone's speaker, the translator talks slowly, filling in the gap in time before our French distributor launches into another spiel.

"Adrien," I interrupt. "Let's focus on the root of the problem for a moment. When do you need the catalog? Give me a realistic timeframe."

I wait as the translator speaks, French quickly flying between the two, and glance again at my watch. Outside my window, the city lights move, cars driving, office lights turning off, a plane twinkling from its place in the sky. I used to enjoy late nights at the office. I loved the quiet, the productive hours without interruption, my inbox finally worked through, any sleepy spells taken care of via a fifteen minute catnap on the couch. Now, I eye the couch, a sleek modern piece that has gotten more than its fair share of use lately, all of it of the X-rated variety. My phone buzzes, and I glance at the text from Trey.

Jet's ready. Take your time. I've got a call with Frank in ten minutes.

I don't respond to it, moving the cell phone aside and pulling up my calendar, looking at design schedules, and our concepts in progress. It takes another forty minutes to come to a date that pleases Adrien, and another ten minutes to stop his attempt to renegotiate our rate.

By the time I hang up, my head hurts. I move to email, firing off updates to the involved parties, and eye the calendar one last time, mentally moving through all of the pieces, making sure that everything is in place before I push away from the desk. I snag my phone and text Trey back on the elevator ride down.

On my way. France is happy.

I walk through the lobby, smiling at the security guard who unlocks the front door and escorts me to my car. "Have a safe trip, Ms. Martin," he says.

"Thanks, John." I open the door and duck into the car, giving him a small wave before shutting the door. I've left this building so many times, heard that parting line so often I could recite it in my sleep. Would he stumble when I returned? Would the first time, the first utter of my new name, sound odd?

I wrap my fingers around the steering wheel and the diamond glints at me. I press down on the clutch and shift the car into reverse, the growl of the engine giving me my first shot of relief. Everything is taken care of. Everything is in place. I back up carefully, then pulling forward and toward the front gate, my nerves loosening by the time I get on the freeway, heading to the airport. I call Jess and my mother, a short conference call filled with teasing giggles and the threat of a surprise visit. I threaten them with bodily harm, then promise to see them as soon as we return.

Three weeks off. Tahiti, in one of those tiki huts set out in the brilliant blue waters of the South Pacific. Three weeks where I would become his wife and we would sip frozen drinks, dance on the sand, skinny dip in that gorgeous water, and get a head start on baby-making. Would the company survive? Two years ago, the answer would have been a resounding *no*. One year ago, I'd have worried the entire time. Now, I feel confident in our team, in our new managers, in the systems and relationships that we've spent these years building.

When I step from the car at the airport, I leave my briefcase and laptop in the trunk, taking only my wallet and passport, my step light as I move through the private airport, the stairs of the jet down, beckoning me. There is movement inside, and then he is there, at the top of the stairs, smiling down at me, and everything in my chest swells.

I'd never believed in fairytales, but this man—he is my prince, my future, my everything.

Him

We take the jet to San Francisco, then get on a huge Airbus, and all of the in-flight amenities don't make up for the fact that I have to behave for nineteen hours, an impossible feat when next to her. She's helping out the cause, especially right now, her mouth gaping open in a most unattractive way, a thin line of drool leaking from the right side of her mouth. I smile, and carefully reach around her, pressing the buttons on her seat until it is fully reclined, her mouth closing, head rolling to one side. I do my best to cover her with a blanket, then recline my own seat, moving onto my right side until I am facing her.

Even now, she terrifies me. Even as I know she accepts my past, she accepts my love, and returns it all. Will I ever believe that it is real? Will I ever be secure that I won't lose her? Or will it only get worse? Is that how love works? Is it more painful the harder you fall? Do you worry more with each additional blessing? I can fight for our love, I can work to be the best husband, the best friend, the best father that I can—I can control those aspects of our marriage. But there will be a thousand more I can't. I can't force her to love me as strongly in ten years as she does now. I can't control if her heart gets bored and finds someone else. I can't control drunk drivers, or freak accidents, or prevent illness from finding her. I can't guarantee that this one moment—her face against the pillow, hand limp against her lap—isn't the last we will have.

I know that it's morbid; I get that it's not rational. Yet, that's the fear that dominates my thoughts. I reach out and wrap my hand through hers, her fingers tightening for a moment. Her eyes open, and there is a drugged moment of awakening, then she smiles.

She smiles and damn—my heart almost breaks from the hit. If there is a way to love a woman more, it must kill a man. She whispers that she loves me, and as I repeat the words back, they feel so inadequate.

If our love was lingerie, it'd be a corset, one laced so tightly that it takes your breath.

If our love was lingerie, it would be drawn on her skin with ink, a tattoo designed to bend and grow with her.

If our love was lingerie, it would be a see-through lace that would share everything while still teasing the hell out of both parties.

If our love was lingerie, it'd be leather, thin strips of binding that could withstand a hundred years of war and peace, fights and love-making. It would yield and give, yet never rip or break. It would be built to last, to wear forever.

If our love was lingerie, it would never come off.

epilogue

five years later

When she comes into the office, I can't stop staring. It doesn't matter if I am elbow-deep in issues, or in the midst of a meeting. Today, when the door opens and she is there, I stop mid-sentence. "Excuse me," I say to the room. I meet her eyes and smile, dropping to my knees on the carpet and calling her name.

Kate releases her hand, and Olivia toddles forward, her footing still a little wobbly, her chubby hand outstretched as she moves toward me. She has her mother's smile, her mother's confidence, and she giggles in the moment before she reaches my arms, her excited shriek muffled against my chest as I pick her up. I meet Kate's eyes and she grins, her other hand full, the newborn hand fisting the front of her shirt. I move toward them both and kiss her first, lingering over her mouth before turning to Baby Trey. I gently kiss the top of his soft head as Kate apologizes to the room. I ignore them, looking into Olivia's eyes, grinning as her hands find my cheeks and gently pat them. When Kate moves toward the door, I lower Olivia to the floor, accepting the high five that she enthusiastically offers.

"We'll be in your office," Kate whispers, and pulls the door open, propping it with her butt as she waits for Olivia to move through it. She waves at me and Olivia mimics the motion, turning and wiggling her fingers at me, a move that makes both Kate and me laugh. Our eyes meet and my heart twists. In my wallet, I have a list of the things that I once loved most about her. A list of ways that she blew me away. The list is old—one I wrote on the back of a napkin six or seven years ago. I wrote it before we were together, before Stephen, back when I was struggling with my feelings and whether or not I had a chance with her. I found the list when I was looking for an old business card, and had felt a wave of nostalgia, looking back through the things that I had once cherished most about her. The list misses everything I would now fill it with. The way that she curls into my body during the night. The look of pride on her face when our children do something amazing. The type of mother she is, the fiercely protective way she loves our family, and leads it in a way that puts Marks Lingerie to shame. The fearless way she loves without hesitation. I spent the first year of our relationship afraid, while she dove in deep and never looked back. Her ability to switch from mother to executive seamlessly. The way that motherhood has softened her stress but strengthened every other seam of her makeup.

She smiles, and I can't look away.

author's note

At the end of each book, when I finish the last sentence and save the file, I feel a little sad. It's a contented sort of sadness - like the drive home from a great vacation. At that point, I've spent months in the lives of these characters, and it is sometimes hard to tell them goodbye. It was especially hard to leave Trey and Kate. I could have kept writing their scenes for weeks. There were so many moments in their relationship that I wanted to capture. And it was hard for me to determine the balance between what was needed for the story, and what would have bogged it down. My biggest fear as an author is boring the reader. And sometimes that fear can negatively affect the story—I rush through it at lightning speed. That was how the first draft of this book was - a quick race through Trey and Kate's story. The second and third draft went back and tried to fill in the gaps, tried to show the important moments that both marked passages of time *and* showed the progression of their relationship.

But even now, I am second-guessing some of my deletions. Even now, with release just days away, I am writing new scenes for this couple. If you want to see the new content I've written, go to www.alessandratorre.com/lilmore/. Please note, these aren't edited or proofed, so please forgive their rough nature.

If this is the first book of mine that you have read, awesome! I hope you enjoyed it. At the end of this note is a guide that might help you pick your next read of mine.

If you are a loyal reader of mine, thank you so much! I appreciate your support more than you will ever know. Please recommend Love in Lingerie to your friends. Your referrals allow me to write full-time and bring you more books!

If you would like to sign up for my newsletter, or be notified on my next release, please go to www.alessandratorre.com/newsletter/. If you would like to follow me on social media and get instant writing updates, sneak peeks, and more, click on the social media links below.

Facebook: www.facebook.com/alessandratorre0/
Instagram: www.instagram.com/alessandratorre4/
Twitter: www.twitter.com/readalessandra/
Goodreads: www.goodreads.com/author/show/6452845.Alessandra_Torre

Looking for another read? Good news - I have plenty to choose from! For links go to my website www.alessandratorre.com.

Other similar books:
- Hollywood Dirt. (NYT Bestseller) When Hollywood comes to a small town to film, its lead actor clashes with a local outcast. (In production to be a movie!)
- Blindfolded Innocence. (First in a series) A college student catches the eye of Brad DeLuca, a divorce attorney with a sexy reputation that screams trouble.

Sexier Reads:
- Black Lies. (NYT Bestseller) A love triangle with a twist that readers couldn't stop talking about. You'll be hating this heroine until the moment you fall in love with her.
- Sex Love Repeat. A woman dates two men at once - an arrangement they are both fine with. They live unaware of the stranger that watches their lives.
- Moonshot. (NYT Bestseller) Baseball's hottest player has his eye on only one thing—his team's 18-year-old ballgirl.
- Tight. Love, sex, and missing women. Lives intersect and secrets are unveiled in this dark romance.
- Mrs. Dumont. (Kindle Unlimited) When a stripper marries a rich stranger, life as a trophy wife is not anything like she expects.

Other Genres:

- The Girl in 6E. (first in a series, erotic suspense) A sexy internet superstar hides a dark secret: she's a reclusive psychopath.
- Love, Chloe. (Chic-lit) A fallen socialite works for an heiress, dodges an ex, and juggles single life in the city that never sleeps.

Made in the USA
San Bernardino, CA
01 August 2017